TEMPTATION

Carter moved from the door and followed Delcia to the family room where she was playing *The Temptations* on the CD player. Several lit candles illuminated the room, their flames flickered and the honeysuckle aroma filled the air.

He had to fight the desire that stirred within him. The moment she'd opened the door, he'd inhaled the sweet scent of her sweet, perfumed body. Her loose hair flowed around her shoulders. She wore a sleeveless sheath that ran from her shoulders to her toes. He wondered what she wore underneath. The thought made his blood run hot.

Delcia glanced at him uncertainly. "I'll be right back," she finally said, backing toward the hallway.

Carter caught her arm before she could escape. "You aren't going to change, are you?"

"Yes," she whispered.

"Don't," he said, perusing her from head to toe.

He glanced into her eyes—eyes that were glassy and bright with wanting and desire.

"We . . . can't," she said as her tongue came out to wet her lips.

He stroked her arm. "Delcia, I've been waiting . . ."

For tonight, Carter wouldn't think of the many dilemmas he faced. Tonight was his time with Delcia.

SHATTERED ILLUSIONS

Candice Poarch

ARABESQUE

BET BOOKS

BET Publications, LLC
www.bet.com
www.arabesquebooks.com

ARABESQUE BOOKS are published by

BET Publications, LLC
c/o BET BOOKS
One BET Plaza
1900 W Place NE
Washington, D.C. 20018-1211

All Kensington Titles, Imprints and Distributed Lines are available at special quantity discounts for bulk purchases for sales promotions, premiums, fund-raising, educational, or institutional use. Special book excerpts or customized printings can also be created to fit specific needs. For details, write or phone the office of the Kensington special sales manager: Kensington Publishing Corp., 850 Third Avenue, New York, NY, attn: Special Sales Department, Phone: 1-800-221-2647.

BET Books is a trademark of Black Entertainment Television, Inc. ARABESQUE, the ARABESQUE logo and the BET BOOKS logo are trademarks and registered trademarks.

First Printing: November, 2000

10 9 8 7 6 5 4 3 2 1
Printed in the United States of America

Acknowledgments

A special thank you to Sue Schiro and Ethel Givens, who have been a tremendous help.

Prologue

Their green camouflage fatigues blended perfectly with the budding hues of the damp and muggy March North Carolina forest. The crunch of boots on the ground and the popping of paint-pellet guns permeated the air and frightened hardy winter birds. In a flurry of feathers, the birds fluttered away. Squirrels frantically searched for new hiding spots every time the guns fired off.

Grease paint smeared across his face, he snuggled behind a dead log and melted into the scenery. He wondered why the hell anyone would choose an imitation military camp for a bachelor party and wished he could hightail it out of there just like the birds. But he couldn't leave until the meeting. Where was he? He'd seen several gun toting guys charging around, but not the one he was waiting for.

Quickly, he covered himself with green brush, hiding himself even more. If he lived through this, he'd go into seclusion to give himself time to think about who was after him. What had possessed him to agree to meet here?

The staccato snap of running feet drew his attention. Grown men fired at each other as they played war games. While the rest of the members of the bachelor party enjoyed the mens' sports, he preferred to continue his search. It had taken him years to get this far. Yet, there was still so much to uncover.

Two shots rang out a hundred yards north of him. Sickly red paint splashed on the tree five yards to his left, but he didn't see anyone over there. He focused on the bushes next to the beech tree for several seconds before he glanced in the direction from where the shot was fired.

Fools. They were probably drunk enough to shoot at any-thing by now. Rabbits, squirrels, shadows, as well as each other. Good thing there was only paint in their guns and not live ammunition.

His ears perked and he glanced at the bushes. Someone was approaching from the direction of the paint-splattered tree. He hunkered closer to the logs, remaining silent and keeping a vigil. Sporadic shots sounded out around him several yards off, but he didn't move. His eyes never wa-vered. Sweat trickled down his face on this unseasonably warm day and yet the T-shirt he wore beneath the fatigues clung to his uncharacteristically cold skin.

Slowly he raised his rifle and aimed toward that spot. Someone was definitely there. He wondered if the person was part of the bachelor party or some hunter trespassing. Should he shoot and scare him off or keep still and hope the person would conclude no one was there and go away? He relaxed a bit. Only members of the party were admitted into this location.

The men with the party were impatient. They wouldn't wait this quietly in one spot. Most were from the city and this was their first foray into war games.

He started to ease back. On TV everyone moved slowly and quietly, but every time he moved, the brush and bram-bles snapped beneath him. Finally, something moved near the tree. A bunch of leaves attached to the man's hat hid most of his face—the face of a stranger. He scuttled back even faster.

The man with a red armband stood, pointing a gun at him.

He managed to gain the cover of a tree that wasn't quite wide enough to hide him completely. "Who are you?" he asked.

The man approached him, saying nothing. He walked closer and closer, the ground cover crackling under his booted feet.

Why didn't he shoot the paint-pellet gun and be done with it? An eerie sense of foreboding crashed through him.

He raised his own rifle holding blue paint pellets and fired.

Royal blue splattered on the man's green fatigues but he didn't fall out as he was supposed to or go back to the camp for another life. He continued to advance, barely staggering from the impact of the paint.

He fired at the helmet, the paint skimming across the top.

Barely escaping, the man ducked, hit the ground, aimed and fired. Like a scene from a script, the whole event had occurred within seconds.

A bullet struck him in the chest. The force crashed him to the ground. The warmth staining his fatigues was his own blood seeping out, not the red paint from the opposing team's paint pellets. The man came closer and he knew this was the end for him. But suddenly, someone shouted and the man melted away, blending into the scenery.

He put a hand to his chest and lifted it to his face. It had never occurred to him that someone would try to kill him here.

Now he'd never meet his real father or his mother's family. He'd never discover why he had been adopted. And he'd never know why he was murdered—or who killed him.

At least no one knew about Delcia and their baby. He'd

*destroyed all her correspondence. She'd think . . . Please,
he pleaded, don't let her try to contact him again. Then
he smiled. He had a baby girl who lived more than a hundred miles away on Coree Island. It was a lark that had
taken him to the small island off North Carolina's Crystal
Coast a year ago. That was when he'd met her.*

A teammate rushed toward him. "My God, no! No!"

The anguished voice drew him back to the present and
the pain exploding through his chest. Slowly his eyes focused
on a familiar face. "My pocket. Take the keys and the letter.
Read it."

The teammate put a hand to his chest as if the action
would prevent the life from flowing out of him.

"Take the letter and go! Now. You'll know . . ." he whispered around the fire in his chest. ". . . what to do. It's
too late for me. Go now!" It took all his strength to say
those few words. His tongue felt thick and dry.

"I'm calling medevac."

"No! Go!"

"I can't leave you here like this."

"Do it . . . for my baby. There's only you." He tried to
lift his arm to shove the man away, but he was too weak.

The man hesitated, then searched his pockets until he
found the items and tucked them into his own pockets. He
heard someone approaching. Looking around, he noticed
it was Ansel, a surgeon. Now he could leave, knowing the
injured man would get the best of care.

"Over here," the teammate called out.

"What's going on?" Ansel asked.

"David's been shot for real," he said averting his face.

"Damn." He ran to the fallen man and stooped, tearing
the shirt apart.

He noticed the fallen man's mouth form, "Go."

He heard more approaching footsteps and he backed to-

ward the trees, the anguish on his face a living thing. He turned back, squeezed his hand, rose and ran off. . . .

The tension drained out of him as he heard footsteps disappear.

He didn't know how long he lay there, thinking about Delcia and their daughter while hearing sporadic shots fire and feeling Ansel work on him. Finally, he heard someone drawing near.

"Hey, Dave!" somebody yelled.

He tried to answer but only a croak emerged.

"Dave?" The same voice approached him. "Come on, man. What the hell is going on?"

Ansel snapped an order. The man stood and obeyed.

The voices faded farther and farther away, and suddenly his eyelids grew too heavy to keep open.

One

Delcia Adams rushed into the Coree Island Convenience and Gift Store, and headed straight to the office to stash her purse into her desk drawer. She always experienced a kind of joy entering this building and seeing the view of the campground she, Bruce, and her brother had built up from two tiny shower stalls and a string of hookups. But lately that jubilance was getting harder to invoke. The tail end of Hurricane Dandy didn't help matters. Thank goodness the destruction to the island was minimum. It could have been a lot worse.

"Your parents all settled in?" Barbara Crump asked. She was one of the campground's few year-round employees.

"Oh, yes." Delcia shut the drawer, tucked her blouse neatly into her jeans and made her way to the door, closing it as she joined Barbara at the reservations desk.

"I know you're glad they're here. Ryan's been complaining again about that leak in his house that he doesn't have time to fix." Methodically, she stacked the check-in cards from the guests who'd arrived two hours ago. "Your dad speaking to you yet?"

"Not yet." Delcia sighed and glanced around. The store was in a separate room from the reservations area. Several guests were milling about in the store but none were here.

"Maybe you should reach out to him. Both of you are kind of stubborn, you know."

Delcia's back went up. Not just anyone could get away with that statement, but Barbara and she had been friends for years. "This impasse was his decision. Besides, if he doesn't want to make amends, there's nothing I can do about it." She grabbed the next day's reservations and drew directions to preassigned campsites with a yellow highlighter. They used breaks in their work schedules to work on the next day's paperwork. It made check-ins much easier.

"I thought for sure he'd loosen up when he held his granddaughter in his arms."

"Oh, he loves Ranetta. Just hates the fact that I wasn't married when I had her."

"She's so precious, she'd steal a thief's heart."

Delcia smiled. "Can't argue with you there. Of course, being the mom, I'm a little prejudiced." But this was Coree Island in North Carolina, an area off the Atlantic Coast that came kicking and screaming into the twenty-first century. Old beliefs died hard here. Delcia glanced out the floor to ceiling windows flanking the storefront. Cars passed in procession. "The ferry has landed. The big rush will start soon." Even as she said it, an RV slowly pulled into the driveway, but Delcia's mind drifted to her father.

As much as she loved seeing her parents, the tension her father persisted on sustaining made the visit difficult. Her parents weren't actually due to arrive for another two weeks, but the rare spring storm that had swept through three days ago hastened their trip. Her father was certain that Delcia and her brother would need the extra help to make repairs in the campground. And he was correct in that. But she wasn't certain that the tension his presence created was worth an extra pair of hands.

If there was one thing that her father had taught her as a child, it was that they were a God-fearing family and there were certain actions that weren't acceptable, even in these modern times. *Just because the world is going to hell in a handbasket doesn't mean that you children have to pick up the handles and carry it along* were his favorite words. Delcia had tried to follow in the way that she'd been taught. But now she was thirty-three and grown and lived an adult life. She'd never dreamed that he'd react so negatively to her pregnancy.

Barbara made a tiny choking sound in the back of her throat, drawing Delcia out of her pondering. Paper crackled as she fanned herself with a map.

Frowning, Delcia glanced first at her friend and then toward the window where a man stood beside his RV checking something.

"Girl, will you look at that brother outside?" Barbara muttered under her breath.

Delcia glanced around to assure herself that none of the customers had wandered into this part of the building, then cocked an eyebrow at her friend. "You're happily married, remember?"

"I am, but you're not."

"Been there and done that." Delcia filed a card in place, not about to let some man checking in for a weekend capture her interest.

Barbara rolled her eyes toward the ceiling. "A two month friendship doesn't make you the most experienced woman on the island." Then she sighed. "I know things didn't turn out right with Richard Connally last year, but . . ." She shook her head. "He was so nice. I never thought he'd just disappear like that."

"Just goes to show. You can't tell a man by his cover." Her brisk tone masked the betrayal that still simmered near the surface. She now knew his gentleness had only been a masquerade, and last year he'd worked her like a pro.

She and Richard had become good friends during his many trips to the campground. For two months they'd dated almost every weekend. Just before he left for Africa to do research on rare plant life, she'd fixed him a parting dinner.

She shook her head. It was only one night. How many teenagers had made that comment? *It happened only once.* But she and Bruce, her husband of eight and a half years, had tried for years for a child and they had never been so blessed.

A night of too much wine had left her mellow and thinking of Bruce, and the fact that her friend was leaving. Loneliness crowded in. That night she and Richard had drifted to bed, to a stage they'd never thought to carry their friendship. He'd had the foresight to use a prophylactic, but the protection hadn't worked.

The next day he'd boarded the plane. Most of the previous night had submerged in the wine-induced haze—until she'd missed her period.

She hadn't loved Richard, but she'd felt some warm affection for him and thought the feeling had been reciprocated. But when she'd written and e-mailed him several times about her pregnancy, he'd never responded.

"You can't give up on the whole male race because of one man."

"Barbara, his actions still puzzle me. Why did he return in February if he didn't care about Ranetta?"

At a loss for words, Barbara shook her head.

"Then, he said he had business to take care of, but he'd be back, and he asked that I not contact him." He'd asked her to marry him when he returned. Delcia had declined. They didn't love each other. But he'd asked her to wait to decide.

Delcia had complied, but when he'd returned a month later with his friends, he acted as if he didn't know her. He was also using the alias, David Washington.

"I've had mine," Delcia said. If nothing else, the experience taught her that no man could replace her beloved Bruce. Bruce had been as honest as they came. Delcia inhaled a shaky breath, holding in the pain. He'd died three and a half years ago, but sometimes at night she could almost feel his arms around her, still picture his easy smile, or remember their conversations just before they'd drift to sleep.

There were many fond memories, all right. Like the way he'd stayed up nights after the day's work was done, carving the welcome sign hanging out front. When she'd been depressed because, as hard as they tried, they'd never had children together, he secretly carved another sign stating "Our Love is Enough" that even now hung on her bedroom wall. She put a hand to her stomach, thinking of his thoughtfulness and the love that burned between them like hot coals. God, how they'd loved.

Delcia closed her eyes against the memories. By now, she should be over him completely. The tears had dried up long ago, but that sense of loss and longing for the closeness they'd shared in their years of marriage at times still clutched her chest like a clenched fist. A year older than she, he'd been her high-school sweetheart.

It had all started when he'd awkwardly thrust three roses with the thorns still attached at her and asked her to the prom her junior year. Pricking her fingers, she'd latched onto the gift, unaware of small beads of blood trailing along her hand. The shy quarterback had noticed her and her heart flew straight to her throat. Tongue-tied, she could only stand there and nod. He'd shuffled his feet, looked at the lockers, the ceiling . . . anywhere but at her . . . until finally she'd squeaked out a "Yes."

Delcia plucked a tissue off the desk and dabbed at her eyes before the tears could spill. She darn well wasn't going to turn on like a faucet anymore. But since that day, there wasn't a part of her life that Bruce hadn't shared.

Barbara's sharp inhalation forced Delcia to focus through the huge, crystal-clear multi-paned window and to the bronze man, standing at least six feet. The North Carolina twilight cast mysterious shadows on him as the swift wind plastered his shirt against his chest.

"Umm-uh. Look at that T-shirt hugging his chest and those jeans molding . . . Lord, child, don't get me started on that face, carved in granite. He's a serious one."

Delcia glanced around to make sure none of the guests had crept in while they were talking about this man like a couple of teenage girls ogling over a football star. "We're too old for this."

Barbara's mouth hung open. "Speak for yourself. I'm not blind, girlfriend, and neither are you," she whispered, gawking at the man. Work was all but forgotten.

"You should be."

"I'm still thinking of you. I've got mine tucked away nicely at home, waiting for me right now." She walked closer to the window. "I hope that one's here for a nice long stay. Maybe he'll get you out of the mood you've been in lately."

"The man probably has a wife and five children outside in a camper, all of them eager to pitch a tent." She ignored her friend's reference to her frame of mind and focused her attention around the room. Everything was in place. The polished pine floors shined so bright they sparkled. The huge stone fireplace with its duck and goose carvings on the mantle had not a speck of dust. Nature and seascape paintings by local artists hung on rough wooden walls and fit the rustic decor perfectly. She snatched a stray pen from the high countertop. Chaotic voices merged through the wide arch leading to the store area that was now teeming with shoppers.

Her brother, Ryan, along with Bruce and she, had built this place with their own hands a decade ago, using the knowledge Bruce had gained working in construction.

"He's sure got the stamina, all right," Barbara

said, forcing Delcia's attention to the man. "But I don't see a wedding band."

"Girl, you need to stop! Plenty of men don't wear their wedding bands." But Delcia had to agree, as she resisted the urge for a closer look, that most men didn't look that good in simple blue jeans and a T-shirt.

"Oh! He's coming inside. I'll let you check him in. Go for it, girl."

"Are you crazy?"

"Just a romantic. Hell, there's hope for you yet." Barbara patted Delcia on the hand and moved from the desk.

As the first one in line, the man had no option but to head straight for Delcia.

Never again, she thought even as she smiled a polite greeting and straightened her name tag. "Welcome to Camp Coree."

The man wasn't exactly gorgeous as much as there was such an imposing presence to him. A presence as stealthy as fog creeping into the island's damp night air.

"Good evening, Delcia," he said. The smile on his lips belied the wintry cast in his obsidian eyes. "A reservation for Carter Matthews, please."

There was something about him beyond his looks . . . an edginess, a toughness, and something more that Delcia couldn't quite put her finger on. The craggy edges undoubtedly drew women like flies. She scrolled through the reservations and pulled his package.

"You have a hookup for your RV near the water." She yanked out a map and spread it on the countertop. "Your space is number one twenty-six. You have complete hookups with water, electric and sewer." When he leaned closer to view the map, she inhaled his fresh woodsy scent, a light mixture of cologne and him. "May I interest you in a cable connection?"

Carter shook his head. "Too much to do to watch TV."

"The directions are highlighted for you in yellow." She pointed to the X. "You are here." She continued with the spiel she repeated several times a day. "Just turn left out the parking lot. In a half mile, you'll see a sign for Waterfront Path. Turn right and drive to the end of the path." She tucked the map back into the envelope. "Your site is in a very quiet area, just as you requested." She handed him the signature card. He completed the information, and passed her his credit card.

Taking it, Delcia ran it through the credit card machine and handed him an envelope filled with information about the camp.

"Our newsletter tells of our upcoming events through September. Weekly bulletins are placed on the desk on Friday mornings. Tomorrow we have a chili cook-off. The proceeds benefit the fire department and the teen center," she said. "Here are a few brochures, but there are more on the stands across the room. Is this your first trip to our island?" she asked him. Looking into his eyes, she recognized what had eluded her before. He looked like a man who'd seen enough to last a lifetime. She guessed he was in his mid-thirties, but his eyes looked much older. Underneath the rough exterior was pain he held tightly in check. She knew because she, too, had had hollow, pain-filled eyes when she'd lost

Bruce. Looking at him was like staring in a mirror. But her Ranetta had changed all that for her. Her baby had brought her some measure of happiness and peace. She wondered if he'd lost a wife he dearly loved. Feeling a kinship with him made him seem more human and that softened him in her eyes.

"It is," Carter responded. "I just retired from the service and I'm using the summer to figure out what I'll do next."

Add "lost" to that, Delcia thought. "Well, you've come to the right place. There's great fishing here and plenty for the nature enthusiasts. Sea turtles, hiking, nesting grounds for water fowl. We have a sandy beach on a small stretch on the west of our island. If you have any questions, please contact us. We're open from six to nine all summer." She flashed him what she hoped was the same welcoming smile she extended to every guest. "Enjoy your stay at Camp Coree."

"Thank you." Clutching the envelope in his hand, Carter walked out the door with quick long strides.

She and Barbara worked frantically for the next half hour. Friday was their busiest check-in day since campers usually arrived for an early Saturday morning start.

"His voice is just as sexy as his looks." Barbara returned to the conversation as if Carter had just left. And there was no question of whom she was referring to. "But he needs this vacation. He's one uptight brother. Maybe he'll lighten up while he's here." She thumbed through the signature cards on the desk until she stopped at his. "About as uptight as you."

"You remember his name?" Delcia asked when the woman stopped at Carter's card.

"And so do you."

Delcia did, but wasn't going to admit it.

"Let's see how long he's staying."

"Three months," Delcia said. A few retirees camped at Camp Coree for months.

"Maybe you just ought to get to know him."

Delcia ignored Barbara's raised eyebrow as well as her rumblings. She hoped he'd find some measure of peace on their island.

Carter strolled to the RV, his stomach clenched tight. Opening the door, he staggered into the seat, leaned his arms across the steering wheel and gulped deep breaths.

Was Delcia responsible for his brother's death? And if David had been mesmerized by her, Carter couldn't blame him a bit. Raven hair and midnight eyes should have been ordinary, but she was striking. And he wasn't easily impressed. He could picture the cinnamon-toned woman enticing his brother to his death, or losing himself in the dark pools of her eyes and the curve of her tented lips. He wouldn't begin to think of her voice that probably enraptured David like a spring flower bursting to bloom. Hell, soldiers dreamed about faces like hers when they were thousands of miles from home in godforsaken countries they'd only glimpsed on a map in school.

But none of those things had happened. David had said he'd never met the woman before she'd accused him of having an affair with her. Besides,

David had been dating the same woman for four years. And David wasn't a liar.

A tightness clenched his throat as he thought of his gentle brother dying a violent death. David had only wanted to help the sick. Even at fourteen, he'd nurse wounded animals back to health. Carter had been in the audience when he'd received his medical degree, as proud of his foster brother as he would have been of a blood brother. They'd both drifted from foster home to foster home until at fourteen, first Carter, then three months later David, had finally wound up with Paul and Nadine Roberts. The poor but hardworking couple couldn't afford to adopt the boys, but they promised them a home forever and they'd been true to their word. They extended both their home and hearts to two lost boys. And Carter and David had promised each other to be brothers for life.

Carter leaned back in his seat, his loss, a sharp, palpable saber wound. He closed his eyes against the pain throbbing through him. *Who the hell talked his brother into that stupid military camp bachelor party in some tiny town west of Raleigh?*

Carter had lived through real battles and had no appreciation of grown men running around playing at war.

While he'd been thousands of miles away in Kosovo, defending other people's families, somebody killed the only brother he had. His fingers tightened around the steering wheel. *I'll find the bastard who killed my David,* he vowed.

Carter shoved the key in the ignition and turned it, the motor springing to life. He drove out of the parking lot and forced himself to focus on his surroundings, desperate to dull the red haze hanging over him. Following Delcia's directions, he passed a pool; a fenced-in play area of swings, slides, sand boxes and monkey bars; rows of tents and motor homes, each site with trees, hedges and brush separating them, lending a degree of privacy. Turning down a side road, he passed a large bathhouse discretely tucked into the trees.

Finally veering onto the road where his hookup was located, he found the trees were thicker. He read the orange and blue signs until he found his own site at the very end, about a hundred feet from the water. Carter stopped and gazed for a moment. About fifty feet of trees and low bushes separated him from the marsh grass that grew to the very edge of the bank. Clear blue-gray water rushed past on its way to the ocean.

He pulled directly into his slot between an old shady scrub oak tree and a pine. He wished he was here on vacation and could enjoy nature and even a bit of fishing. David and Paul loved to fish.

He sighed and exited the RV, studying the fading blue sky and the flocks of birds and geese. The view of the water that spread for as far as he could see was breathtaking. The aroma of rotting marsh life mingled with the salty Atlantic and filled his senses.

Surrounded by beauty, Carter wondered again about the diligent, hardworking woman he'd met at the registration desk and the games she was playing.

He had work to do before darkness set in completely. Attaching the hookups to his RV, he found himself swatting at mosquitoes and bluebottles. He raced to unload his motorcycle and park it beside the RV before he was eaten alive. Dodging into the camper, he made a mental note to buy insect repellent from the country store. He opened the window protected with screens to catch the air. It was warm but at least it eased the heat. It also carried in the aroma of grilled fish from a neighboring camp, reminding him that he had missed dinner.

The brochure mentioned a fast-food stand. The trip would give him another opportunity to size up Delcia. The more he saw of her, the more comfortable she'd be with him and the easier to pump her for information.

"Hello there," someone called from behind him. "That bike is something else."

Carter turned at the voice. A six-foot cinnamon-toned man with reddish brown hair was checking out the motorcycle.

The man extended a hand. "Randall Greene."

Carter returned the handshake. "Carter Matthews."

Randall circled the bike, stroking the surface. "Just came to invite you over for some of our fish. The catch was really good today. We've got more than we can eat."

"Thank you," Carter said.

"First time here?" Randall asked.

"It is."

"Be happy to tell you about the best fishing spots if you're interested." Hearing the southern twang in the man's voice, Carter guessed he was from close by. It wasn't quite as thick as Alabama, but still held that distinct resonance.

"I'm interested," Carter said.

"I'm with a couple of friends. We went fishing

today. The water was pretty choppy." He nodded toward the camp across from Carter. "We have plenty."

"It sure smells good," Carter said. "I just may take you up on that." He swiped at the pesky mosquito that landed on his arm.

"Best fish you'll ever taste. See you in a half hour." He waved and ambled on.

Watching Randall stroll back to his camp, Carter got on his motorcycle and rode toward the store, thinking what a friendly lot these campers were.

Moving down the grocery aisle, he found the insect repellent and started to buy one can. He thought of the three months he'd be here, picked up several instead, and turned.

In his path stood a woman of about eighty wearing a long navy cotton dress piercing him with wizened eyes.

"Good evening," Carter greeted her.

She remained silent, steadily watching him. "Dangerous tides follow you," she finally said in a low voice. "Be careful."

"Grandma? Are you ready?" Carter heard the younger voice before he saw a woman appear at the end of the aisle near the canned vegetables.

The older woman pierced him with one last glare and frowned. Turning, she shuffled toward her granddaughter.

"Come on, let's go." The younger woman gently took her grandmother's elbow. In her other hand she carried a paper sack.

Carter watched them as they left. He shook his

head and carried his basket to the cash register, the woman's warning reverberating in his mind. Bad tides had already come.

The register was being run by a man whose name tag flashed "Ryan."

"How are you?" Ryan said.

"Hello," Carter said. "Your mosquitoes ran me here."

The man laughed. "They get pretty pesky in the early mornings and evenings."

"You got a pretty neat set up here," Carter said, glancing around.

"We like it." There was pride of ownership in his voice. Carter remembered the ring on Delcia's finger and guessed Ryan must be her husband, although he didn't wear a ring. Her having had an affair with David spoke volumes about her morals. He wondered if maybe Delcia and Ryan had decided to fleece the good doctor, his brother.

"How many years have you been here?"

"Twelve. And growing bigger each year. Can I get anything else for you?" Ryan asked, the smile and easy camaraderie firmly in place.

Carter shook his head, no. "Thank you. There is one thing. The older woman who just left."

"Mrs. Grant. She's the daughter of one of the first group of lighthouse keepers on the Outer Banks. Our waters are known as the graveyard of the Atlantic. If you can catch her, she would love to regale you with her family's history. The young woman with her is her granddaughter, Dr. Grant. She operates the small island medical clinic."

Carter paid for his purchases. Ryan put them in a plastic bag and handed it to him. "Enjoy your stay."

"I intend to." He grabbed his bag and headed for the door. He eased around a family of four and left the busy store. He hoped his stay wouldn't be long at all. But Mrs. Grant had caught his interest. Why did she make that statement? Carter laughed at himself. Pretty soon, he'll be believing in roots, ghosts, and all the stories and witchcraft the South was famous for.

The phone rang just as Delcia and Ryan were closing the camp store. She shifted her purse to the other hand and picked up the receiver. "Camp Coree," she answered.

She listened to the caller and watched Ryan as he tiredly waited for her to finish. He'd been here since six, the same as she. "I'll send someone right over." She hung up the phone. "Site sixty-seven is having problems with their water lines. I think Andre has gone home for the evening." Andre Anderson was their cousin and head of park maintenance.

Ryan sighed. "I'll check it out. Lock the door and go on home." He headed toward the maintenance shed.

Delcia killed the overhead lights, leaving on the night light. She was two yards from the door when Jenny Shaw entered, the bell tingling.

Surprised, Delcia suddenly stopped. The woman clutched the straps of her huge black purse.

"Is anything wrong Jenny?"

"No, no." She shook her head. Gray streaks had started to show through. When her daughter asked her why she didn't color her hair, she'd responded that she'd earned every gray string in her fifty-two years and they didn't bother her one little bit.

"I just wanted to talk to you a moment."

"Sure, come on in." Delcia turned the light back on and led the nervous woman to one of the chairs flanking the fireplace.

After she'd settled into the cushions, Delcia asked, "What can I do for you? Can I get you a soda? We've cleaned the coffeepots already."

"No, no. I just wanted to ask you . . . with your mom being here and all and wanting to spend time with Ranetta . . ."

"She and my dad will be here for three weeks." Delcia wondered why that would be a problem. They'd visited before without an incident. Jenny got along with them rather well.

Jenny continued her stranglehold on her purse. Delcia wondered if her fingers hurt from clutching the bag so tightly. "I just wondered if I'll still be getting my paycheck."

Delcia suppressed a smile. "Of course you'll get your check. You're still Ranetta's sitter."

Jenny relaxed perceptibly. "I was just worried because I count on my check to pay the bills." She stood and started walking toward the door.

Delcia fell in step with her. "Don't worry about a thing. If you need some time off, just make sure that Mom is available. It won't be a problem. You'll still get your check," Delcia added.

Jenny frowned. "Well, I appreciate it. I've got a doctor's appointment I've been putting off with your being so busy and all."

"Go ahead and make your appointment. I don't want you to take chances with your health."

Delcia locked the building and walked with Jenny to the car. Soon she was driving down the tree-lined drive to her house. It was a beautiful home with wood siding but it was also an enormous amount of work to maintain because of the Atlantic's saltwater.

The house was quiet when she arrived. She was glad that her parents were asleep. Her greeting with her dad had been stilted at best—he still hadn't forgiven her for having Ranetta out of wedlock. Clay Anderson was quick to judge and slow to forgive. The next three weeks were going to be the longest in her life.

Truth be told, Delcia felt a smidgen of anger toward him. She was his daughter after all. Daughters weren't perfect—they were human. Before she could work herself into true anger, Delcia forced the dilemma from her mind and marched to her bedroom.

By the time Delcia showered and got ready for bed, eleven had come and gone. Since she rose at five each morning, she should have been asleep. She counted the weeks until the college students arrived, crossing the days off on a mental calendar. Then her hours would decrease to a normal eight or ten. Now, Ryan and she each burned the candle at both ends, leaving little time for a personal life.

Delcia entered the baby's bedroom and tiptoed to the crib, getting a last glimpse of Ranetta before she turned in for the night. While she watched Ranetta sleep, she wished she could spend more time with her child. Delcia stroked the back of her hand against the baby's cheek. Ranetta stirred and Delcia moved her hand away. Her skin was so warm and soft that Delcia had to resist the urge to pick her up and kiss her. Gently tucking the covers around her, she silently left the room.

God, her eyes felt gritty. It was too late to read the paper. She put it on the table by the recliner and trekked into the kitchen for a glass of water from the fridge. Maybe tomorrow, she thought as she rubbed her stiff neck. Trotting to the family room, she picked up the last of the stuffed toys, tossing them into the toy chest. Then she sank into her favorite overstuffed recliner and put her feet on the ottoman. She was too tired to sleep. She'd just rest a few minutes before she'd climb into bed.

As Delcia closed her eyes, the camper's troubled eyes came into focus. It was the last image she remembered before she fell asleep.

TWO

Monday morning, Carter forced himself out of bed. Goose bumps beaded on his arms. The temperature in the RV had dropped at least twenty degrees overnight. He dragged himself into the minuscule shower and was glad that the room heated quickly from the hot water.

Carter wasn't a stranger to extreme temperatures. It was part of a Navy SEAL's life. That life was behind him now, Carter thought with more than a little regret. Being a SEAL had been more than a tour of duty.

Close contact and dangerous missions made them more like a family. Their lives depended on each other. Men held onto that association with every part of their being. The worst of fates was to have an injury that took you off the team.

Injured SEALS who were recuperating often trained recruits. At Little Creek in Norfolk it wasn't unusual to see injured SEALs limping around, trying to heal so that they could pass the test and re-enter their unit—often to no avail.

All wasn't lost with Carter, though. His captain, who retired five years ago, heard that Carter was leaving the military and offered him a position in his international security firm. Carter hadn't accepted but the man had left the invitation open. Carter didn't quite know what he would do, but he was resigned to take the offer once this business about David was completed.

He thought about his upcoming appointment with the detective who was working on David's case. He hoped the man had more information than he offered when Carter had called him last week, which was just about nil.

After a speedy shower, he dressed and used the repellent liberally. Opening the door to the tiny closet, he pulled out a jacket and slipped it on. Zipping it up, he exited his temporary home and was instantly serenaded by the birds. He noticed that several campers had already headed out with their boats.

The surroundings pulled Carter back to his childhood. The Roberts would take them on camping trips at least twice a year. Nadine hated living out of doors, but she insisted that everyone go on the vacations. It was years before Carter realized that those were the only vacations they could afford. Back then, he thought they were just like every other family in the neighborhood.

David had loved those early morning fishing trips in their canoes. Nadine refused to go along. She would stay near camp and explore the area, read a book or crochet. Carter smiled. He'd loved those trips as much as David had. The Roberts had been the first family that he'd gone on vacations with. They'd planned a trip for this summer. Nadine was always thinking of ways to get them together.

He glanced across the path at Randall's site. Everything was quiet over there. Last night, Randall had mentioned that his group would leave at five to spend the day fishing. Carter almost wished he could go fishing, but alone. He didn't care for crowds. He liked his solitude. Of course, the camps they'd visited as children weren't as lavish as these accommodations. They'd contained the bare minimum—cold showers and bathrooms.

Carter glanced at the sky. Not a cloud in sight. The meteorologist predicted the temperature would range in the low seventies, a perfect day for his trip to Greenville. The detective had been out on a case Friday when he'd stopped there. But first, coffee.

Mounting his bike, he started up and imagined the heads springing up in their sleeping bags at the noise. As he coasted by, campers were loitering about at small stoves, brewing their first cups of coffee. Many nodded as he passed. Some were starting out with backpacks strapped to their backs and hiking boots on their feet. He heard children chatter excitedly about their upcoming adventures.

One little boy who looked no older than five, hopped up and down. "Can I ride the turtles, Mom, can I?" he asked repeatedly.

His mom sighed fondly at her child. "It's 'May I.' And no. You may look at them though." Carter guessed they would spend the day on the nature trails Delcia had mentioned.

The ever-present mosquitoes were at it again but kept a safe distance from the repellent he'd donned.

A few minutes later, Carter opened the door to the store, the smell of coffee drawing him. The place was quieter than it had been through the weekend. He made for the table in the corner, poured coffee in a Styrofoam cup, and watched as customers checked into the campground while others shopped for items they needed. Both Delcia and Ryan were working. A young lady who looked to be around twenty manned the reservation desk alone. From the looks of things, the park was only half full and not nearly as busy as it had been during the weekend.

He wondered how much time they had left over to spend with each other.

As Carter sipped on his coffee and warmed himself in front of the fireplace, he thought of eating breakfast there, but settled for a blueberry muffin. The thought of his upcoming trip had taken away his appetite. Perhaps he would eat later at a local restaurant.

He rode to the dock and had only a short wait before the ferry started the boarding process.

His first order of business was a trip to the sheriff's office. A week ago he'd made an appointment to meet the detective in charge of investigating David's case. Yesterday he'd made a second call to another contact, just in case the detective had nothing to offer.

The little town just south of Greenville was an hour's ride from the ferry. The time passed quickly as Carter's mind gravitated to his brother.

Upon entering the police station, Carter was immediately directed to Detective Stubb's desk.

The men shook hands and Carter sat in an uncomfortable metal chair beside the desk. This wasn't one of those upscale offices; they were tucked away in a small room with four other desks. It seemed the sheriff was the only one with a private office. Carter gave Stubb the regards of a navy buddy of his who had attended high school with the detective.

"Your brother was shot with a hunting rifle. Everyone around here has one. We believe that a hunter may have mistakenly roamed into that area and shot him by mistake—then was too afraid to come forward."

"Everyone who hunts needs a hunting license. Have you investigated the hunters in that area that day?"

"We don't know of any. It wasn't hunting season—anyone out there was hunting illegally. It happens all the time. We don't believe it's a deliberate homicide. We've used this on TV for *Crime Watch* and offered a small reward. The area was tramped with so many foot patterns that it was difficult to get any definitive evidence."

Carter thought about the letter he received from his brother telling him that Delcia had accused him of having an affair with her. There was more to this situation than some rogue hunter miscalculating David for a deer. Maybe Ryan thought his wife was fooling around with David.

Stubbs was called from his desk. As the man left the room, Carter glanced around. One other detective was on the phone, his back toward Carter. Carter plucked the folder in front of the detective's chair from the stack of other folders piled on his desk. David's name was on the label.

Carter steeled himself for viewing the photos. Despite his resolve, nothing could prepare him for the impact of seeing David with a hole in his chest and the blood-soaked clothing. He'd sustained a wound that made it impossible for him to survive.

Carter flipped one page after another of photos. The nausea that started in his stomach increased and he swallowed hard. His chest reverberated with pain. The SEALs had taught him to channel pain. *Concentrate on your quest for justice,* he said to himself. *Winning means control.* With a shaky hand, he pulled half a coin on a chain from underneath his T-shirt. Sliding his thumb across its rough surface brought him some small measure of peace. David wore the other half around his neck.

Carter had asked his foster parents about David's coin before he started out on the trip. It hadn't been among his effects. And Carter noticed the chain's absence from the pictures.

Clamping his teeth, Carter swallowed again and continued on until he heard voices. He closed the folder, and returned it to the stack.

When Stubbs seated himself behind his desk, he said, "Sorry about that."

Carter cleared his throat. "Did he die immediately?"

"He lasted a few minutes."

The shot was perfect, designed to kill him. This was no error.

Carter indicated the chain at his neck. "A chain with a coin like this is missing from his effects. Did you find it?"

He shook his head. "We gave the foster parents everything."

Carter thanked the detective, gave him his cell phone number and left.

Walking out the door Carter reflected on the fact that he was the one who had fought in wars around the world. His death wouldn't have been such a shock, maybe even expected. Yet his brother was the one gone.

Carter pulled a piece of torn paper from his wallet and read it. He retrieved his map and drove to Kirk Rice's address. The same navy buddy who had given him the detective's name had offered this contact.

Carter drove to a trailer court and parked his bike in front of a double wide. He was surprised at the tree-lined acreage, strewn with blooming roses and azaleas.

A tall, tan-complexioned man wearing black leather pants and an open vest answered his knock.

"Carter Matthews," he told him. The man stepped back to let him enter.

Clean thick white carpeting covered the living room floor. The furniture: cream leather sofa and chairs with glass-topped tables.

"Joe Bob recommended you," Carter told him.

"He called. What can I do for you?"

Carter passed him a clipping from the newspaper—the story of David's death. "I'm looking for the shooter."

Rice glanced at the article, then at Carter.

"Once I find him?"

"I'd like the name and location."

"It'll cost you," Rice finally said.

"How much?"

He named a figure. "Half now and half when the job's done."

In anticipation of this visit, Carter had bought money along, just in case. He reached into his wallet and counted out the bills, leaving them on the glass-topped table. He gave the man the number to his cell phone and left.

* * *

At one-thirty that afternoon Jenny brought Ranetta by the camp store on her way to pick up diapers and formula.

"I completely forgot," Delcia said, feeling like an
incompetent mother.

"Your plate's too full. Besides, little precious here
is all I do."

Little precious started fussing to get to her mother
as soon as she saw her. "Can you handle things while
I take a short lunch break, Barbara?" Her stomach
had just reminded her about lunch. Where had the
time gone?

"Of course I can."

A high school senior was working with them today,
enabling Delcia to complete other chores.

"I packed lunch for you," Jenny said, patting the
picnic basket she carried on her other arm. "I know
you haven't eaten. I packed enough for Ryan, too.
The two of you are so much alike. You'll work all
day without a thought to your stomach," she admonished.

"Take an hour," Barbara said, "like normal folks
do."

Delcia thought of the pitifully few minutes she
had spent with her child yesterday and decided to
do just that.

"I'm going to run into town," Jenny said. "I forgot to ask your mom to pick up some things when
she and your dad went to Morehead City to pick up
supplies for your uncle's roof."

Delcia dug into her pocket for money.

Jenny waved her on. "I took cash out of the petty
cash drawer at the house."

Taking her baby from Jenny, Delcia snuggled Ranetta against her face. "Don't you smell good."

Ranetta laughed and wrapped her arms around Delcia's head as she kissed her.

"Jenny must have just given you a bath." Smiling, Delcia put the basket on her arm and went through the grocery area talking to her child.

Ranetta pumped her feet and squealed when she saw Ryan. He immediately plucked the baby out of Delcia's arms, lifted her in the air, and tickled her tummy with his face. Ranetta fell into a fit of giggles.

"On your way to lunch?" he asked Delcia.

"We are. Jenny packed enough for you. Join us."

The smile left his face. "Take the rest of the day off and spend it with Rae." He'd long ago shortened her name.

"Wish I could. But you know as well as I that I can't take the time off."

He sighed. "I wish you could spend more time with her."

Delcia laid her hand on his arm, touched all over again by his thoughtfulness. What sister could ask for more?

"It'll get better. Take her on out and I'll grab a quilt."

He took the basket off her arm and started out back.

Delcia stopped by the office, dragged an old quilt out of the cabinet, and went out back to a tiny closed off area they'd built so the employees had someplace to eat during their lunch break.

Hedges and trees grew around the perimeter of the chain-link fence, lending a softer, more natural view. Two picnic tables were scattered on the fenced-in, grassy, twenty square-foot area. Small, but at least they could get a little privacy and Delcia could play on the grass with Ranetta under the scrub oak tree.

Ryan sat on a corner of the bench, playing with Ranetta. Delcia spread out the quilt on the freshly cut grass. Then she plunked the basket on one end. Ryan ambled over and sat across from her, putting Ranetta on the quilt between them.

Digging into the basket, Delcia pulled out two chicken sandwiches and two small containers of potato salad.

"Umm."

"A treat I definitely could use."

She passed Ryan a sealed wet napkin and used one herself. Then she took the wet washcloth Jenny had packed, wiped off Ranetta's hands, tied a bib on her, and handed her a teething biscuit. Now that she was teething, she was perfectly content to gum the treat as Ryan and Delcia ate their own lunch.

"I've been thinking that we should talk about hiring someone full time who can take on more responsibility. Will our finances allow it?" Delcia asked before she took a bite of potato salad.

"I think so. The idea's crossed my mind, too. We're also at the point of thinking if we want to expand."

"Do you want to expand?" He was thinking about marriage. LaToya Drew, his soon to be fiancée, wanted him to move to the Triangle area, and he'd just received an offer for an accounting position there. Even with his help, she worked sixteen hour days. Without it . . . the situation didn't bear thinking about.

Still, he had yet to talk to his sister about his plans.

Delcia had assured him that she could run the park alone if they hired on more full-time employees. She knew LaToya was pressuring him to move on. Delcia wouldn't let the park be the cause of contention between him and the woman he loved.

He sighed. "I'm not sure."

She'd asked him before. She wouldn't complicate matters by badgering him about it. Ultimately, the decision was his.

"We're already booked for the next three week-ends. We're definitely going to have to expand this park next winter," he said.

"I've already had to turn some campers away."

"It's recorded in the computer?"

"It's recorded," Delcia assured him. Ryan had rigged up a program to record all the turn away customers to give them an idea of how much expansion their customer base could support.

They finished their lunch quickly. Delcia cleaned up Ranetta and pulled off her messy bib. While Delcia threw the plates and plastic utensils into the trash, Ranetta crawled to Ryan and sat on his lap. He played with her while they talked.

"I need to take some time to go through all that data. Maybe this weekend. Scratch that. LaToya's coming Friday." He glanced at his watch.

"You don't have very much time to spend with her, do you?" Delcia leaned forward and plucked Ranetta out of his arms, planting a kiss on her cheek, then setting her on her lap.

"Not much." He took out a soft rubber toy and squeezed it in front of Rae. The baby reached for it, bouncing on Delcia and squealing with delight.

"Perhaps you can take a day or two during the week when it's slower."

"Maybe later on when we aren't so busy." He stood in one smooth motion. "I've got to get back to work," he said, dismissing the thought. He dropped the toy on the quilt.

Ranetta picked it up in her tiny hands and squeezed.

It was always "maybe later" with them, Delcia thought. Maybe later she'll have more time for her baby. Maybe later Ryan will have more time for his girlfriend. No wonder he was considering leaving. They both needed time for a life.

She chuckled at Barbara's attempts to get her interested in Carter. Even if she were so inclined, what time would she have for him? Maybe later, Delcia thought as she picked up her baby and attempted to teach her patty cake.

Carter made his way back to the island on the noon ferry. He put his helmet on the bike and walked toward the bow to feel the wind. Clutching the rail, the sharp force of the salty air slapped his face. The cry of seagulls called out as they dived for food. As they followed the ferry they gracefully swayed in the air. Breathing in the crisp ocean air, the tightness in his chest lessened by degree.

He saw shadowed trees in the distance, their gnarled branches reaching out. As they approached their destination, slash pine and lob lolly pine trees stood tall behind the marsh grass. They were almost at the island.

Carter made his way to his bike and pulled the

map for directions to the downtown area. One main road, clearly marked, led straight there. He put on his helmet, kicked up the kick plate and rolled to a start.

The trip took less than five minutes and he was surprised to be greeted by well maintained buildings near the waterfront that were clearly designed to impress the tourist trade. Shop owners had busily hammered away to repair the damage caused by a recent storm.

A few tourists roamed the streets, meandering from one quaint shop to the next. Even though Carter was starved, he couldn't eat a thing; but from past experience, he knew the quickest way to the heart of a town was through the diner the locals frequented. He spotted a lone building with a bedraggled sign swinging in the wind that read "Wanda's." It was on the very edge of town, well apart from the other buildings. Carter rode the bike a short distance up the hill to reach it. Even Wanda's hadn't escaped ravishment from the storm. Few tourists entered the building, but many locals rushed in for their noon-time meal, or at least what could be termed rushed for this part of the South. In New York they would be considered to be meandering.

Carter liked the slower pace of the island.

He entered the building, allowing a few seconds for his eyes to adjust to the dim interior.

Tables covered with vinyl red and white checkered tablecloths held condiments, but no candles or fragrant flowers. The chairs of substantial oak, needed refinishing more than a decade ago. Several men were seated at the bar.

"I'll be right with you." An efficient hostess led a backpack carrying couple who were in front of him. Tourists, Carter surmised.

"I'll just take a seat at the bar."

The woman smiled and led the couple to their table.

Carter headed for the only empty chair at the bar. Once there, he glanced at the house specials advertised in a plastic holder placed between the salt and pepper.

"Well, hello there." A woman who wore her hair in a French twist slapped a menu in front of him. "I'm Akela. What can I get for you to drink?"

"Coffee," Carter said, glancing up. The nutmeg-toned woman wore cherry red lipstick and used a light hand on eyeliner and mascara. They served to enhance her already attractive features, but he wasn't taken with her. To his consternation, he couldn't get Delcia out of his mind.

"The special's red snapper today. Came in fresh off the boat this morning. Soup's fish chowder. Take a look at the menu and I'll be right back with your coffee." She trekked to the other end of the bar, expertly snatching two plates from the serving window along the way and planting them in front of waiting customers. She struck up a brief conversation with them before making her way back to Carter with his coffee.

Carter gave up on the menu and placed it back in the holder. While she filled his cup, Carter told her, "I'll have the special."

"Would you like rolls or corn bread with that?" she asked, her pencil flying across the tiny pad.

"Corn bread," Carter answered. He had a true appreciation for fine Southern corn bread.

Leaving Carter on his own, she pinned the order on the carousel and greeted another guest. Carter glanced around the lopsided room. The tourists lingering at some of the tables were easily distinguishable by their attire and the maps and brochures they pored over. Slumped in their chairs, some looked haggard from their morning's excursions, and not too eager to start out again.

"Say, Akela," a voice from the man sitting beside Carter called out.

"What is it, Harry?"

"Bring me a piece of that strawberry pie with a scoop of ice cream, will ya?"

"All right," she hollered back as she turned to the window, pulled Carter's soup out, and deposited it in front of him. "Hope you enjoy it. Let me know if I can get you anything else now."

"Thank you," Carter said. She went to fix Harry's dessert. In no time, she slid a plate heaping with luscious red strawberry pie and ice cream covered with whipped cream under Harry's nose.

"Willow Mae throw you out the house again, Harry?" Akela asked.

A round of giggles emerged from the other patrons at the bar.

Harry gave them a sour look. "Women," Harry said, shaking his head. "Who can figure? They've always got something to fight about."

Akela left and Harry leaned over his plate, dismissing everyone and obviously enjoyed his fare.

Carter listened in on one of Akela's conversations as he ate his fish chowder. It seemed that the woman was the eyes and ears of the island community, soaking up gossip like a sponge and divulging it just as quickly.

Before Carter knew what happened, he'd eaten the entire bowl and Akela exchanged the empty soup bowl for his lunch plate, steam rising from the food.

"Can I give you a refill on that?" she asked.

"No, but it was delicious." Carter started in on the snapper that must have still been squirming seconds before it landed in the hot grease, it tasted so fresh. The hush puppies melted in his mouth. The greens were loaded with enough grease to fry a chicken, but they tasted excellent. The potato salad—well, he could only compare it to Nadine's.

The bell tingled in the background as customers came and went, and Carter enjoyed his fare. No wonder Harry ate silently.

When Carter finished, he wiped his mouth with the paper napkin, leaned back in his chair, and put his napkin on his plate.

Harry nursed his coffee, in no hurry to leave. Carter guessed that if he'd been thrown out, he really didn't have anyplace to go.

"First time on our island?" Harry finally asked.

"Yes, it is."

Harry looked to be in his late sixties. "Staying at the camp?"

Carter nodded.

"The land's been in the family for near a hundred years now." He leaned back into his seat and plucked up a toothpick near his plate.

Carter thought it must be wonderful to be able

to recount one's family back so far—to have family living around you.

"Looks prosperous. It was pretty busy this weekend." Carter said.

"Getting into their busy season." He sucked on the toothpick. "Delcia and Ryan are my youngest brother's kids. They built that camp with Delcia's husband. Started out small, but it soon grew like lightning." He cackled and hit his leg. "That Delcia's a smart one. She finished college the same year Ryan finished high school. They started building and come spring, they had business pouring in. They built more each winter til her husband passed away three and a half years back." Harry shook his head. "Just she and Ryan runs it now."

Immediate pleasure shot through Carter when he discovered Ryan was her brother. Then he frowned, remembering she might be guilty of murder. He was getting ahead of himself. He couldn't afford to think below his belt. And Delcia was just the kind of woman to divert his thoughts in the wrong direction. "That's sad," he finally responded.

"It was that. Bruce grew up right here." He looked into space, reliving memories. "Best gow'derned quarterback the team's ever had. Haven't had a season like that since," Harry lamented. "How long are staying at the camp?"

"Three months. Just retired from the service."

"I'm a service man, myself. Did a couple of tours in Nam."

"No kidding?" Carter said and shook his head. "I've seen more than my share."

Harry nodded in commiseration. "The wife didn't understand I needed a little time to myself when I came home. Got madder than a wet hen when I took off for a spell."

A woman waiting—anyone waiting—for his return, would have pleased Carter immensely. Then the image of Delcia sprang to mind and wouldn't leave. "They tend not to understand," Carter said, pushing Delcia from his thoughts.

Harry chuckled and slapped the bar. "That's the understatement of the century. You got an old lady?"

Carter shook his head. No one was waiting for him anywhere.

"Can I get you a piece of pie?" Akela interrupted their conversation.

"I'm stuffed. Maybe next time."

She shoved the check in front of him. "Well, don't be a stranger, you hear?"

"I won't." He left her a hefty tip, said good-bye to Harry, and took the bill to the cash register to pay.

He'd let Harry get used to him and Harry had volunteered information. A sneaking suspicion told him Harry would be there most days during lunch. Carter would lunch there every day until he gathered all the information he needed.

Carter decided to go by the camp store on his way to the RV. The building was bustling with activity. He watched Delcia enter with a basket on her arm and a baby on her hip. The baby was grinning and so was Delcia. They made a lovely, happy pair. Then she kissed the baby and handed her to an older lady. "I'll try to have dinner with her. Thanks for bringing her by, Jenny." She leaned over and kissed the baby again. "Mom's going to miss you, sweetheart." She waved as the older woman walked toward the door, carrying the child.

Carter held the door for them. As they passed, he looked closely at the child, who'd had her eyes on Delcia. The baby gazed at him with David's unusual large green eyes.

"Thank you." The older woman smiled at Carter as she exited the building.

Time passed before Carter pulled his gaze from the baby. "You're welcome," he finally croaked. He followed their retreat as they neared a Ford. The woman opened the passenger door and secured the baby into the car seat.

The baby was looking straight ahead. But the eyes were seared in Carter's memory.

"That's Ranetta," a soft voice murmured in back of him.

David's child. Carter already knew that. The question was, how was he going to handle this?

Three

The wind had picked up when Carter started back. He parked the bike but he was much too restless to hide away in the RV. Storing the helmet and jacket inside, he began his journey along the water's edge. He noticed how the Spanish moss covered the oak trees like a lacy lady's shawl.

David had dated Louise for years. He'd always been a one-woman man. Not even in high school had David played around as other teenagers had.

David's letter clearly stated he hadn't met Delcia before. And David wasn't a liar. Yet, Carter couldn't forget that David's eyes had watched him through Delcia's baby.

If Carter were to believe what he'd witnessed, then he would have to reevaluate his entire assessment of a brother he had cared for for many years. He knew David. David would never turn his back on his own child or pretend he didn't know this woman—if he indeed knew her. David and he had agreed that providing a secure environment for their offspring would supersede everything else. They'd talked about it incessantly as children and as adults. Because they were raised in the foster care system, David had promised to be godparent to Carter's children and Carter had promised the same to David.

Carter searched for excuses for what he'd witnessed. Could David have been ill the last year? Carter hadn't been around, so if changes had occurred, he wouldn't know.

Louise would know. She had worked with him as well as being his fiancée.

Carter made a mental note to talk to Louise to see if David had exhibited any strange behavior patterns. Was there some genetic disorder in his background? Since David had been adopted, medical information was unavailable.

Carter glanced at the water where birds hovered in the air overhead. Turning, he retraced his steps. Blue-gray water rippled to and fro; lacy moss draped the trees; a child's muted laughter rang in the distance. There was something to be said for the island's serenity.

Carter returned to the RV and reluctantly reached for his cell phone. Goodness knows, he had never cared very much for Louise, but David had had tunnel vision when it came to that woman; he had seen nothing but the best in her. Even as a teenager he'd never been a good judge of character—too trusting.

Louise was a user. But David could never see that side of her. Talk between Carter and Louise would be difficult. Her opinion of him wasn't very high either. After all, Carter wasn't a doctor like David or she.

David had appointed Carter the executor of his estate. Louise had left several messages for him to get on with his duties. There were three doctors altogether in the practice and they had an insurance policy that would pay for the equipment loan and for the mortgage for the office. That move left

Louise and her partner in much better financial shape than they would have been if David was still alive. For this benefit, they were to make payments to Carter and the Roberts for the life of the practice. The remainder of the estate had been left to Carter and the Roberts. Carter decided his share would go to Delcia's child once he was certain David was the father.

Carter could provide for himself. He didn't need David's money, but the baby and their foster parents would. The Roberts were good and decent people who had offered their meager home to David and Carter. Carter and David had paid off their foster parent's mortgage three years ago. Even now, he sent them money from every paycheck even though they asked him not to. They were due for an easier life.

Carter turned off the phone. This wasn't the first time he'd wondered whether Louise had given David a hallucinogen or a drug that would distort his memory and alter his behavior. That David would deny the parentage of his own child was preposterous. That David would willingly have an affair with another woman while he was engaged to Louise was equally ridiculous.

Another thought surfaced. Could David have broken off the engagement with Louise and planned to marry Delcia instead? But the letter said he'd never met her.

Money was a powerful incentive. With the mortgage and expensive equipment for the practice paid off, Louise and her partner were in an excellent position. David's death left them debt free. Louise could afford all the little things she'd always wanted without a huge loan hanging over her head.

Suspects for David's murder: a hunter, Louise, and her partner: And where did Delcia fit in all of this? Was she the innocent she portrayed? One move Carter couldn't delay any longer—he would introduce himself to her as David's brother.

Clay Anderson left his wife at Delcia's and drove Ryan's truck to his oldest brother's house. The news had spread throughout the island that Willow Mae had thrown Harry out of the house again. Pauline had heard it from a friend who she still kept in touch with and she'd heard it from Lord knows where. He shook his head at the island's grapevine.

Harry's arguments with Willow Mae were legendary. Still, Harry had promised to be home to help Clay unload the supplies to repair the roof.

Clay slowed to a crawl and turned into Harry's drive. The road was so full of potholes that in spots he had to drive halfway off the road to miss them. He couldn't tell how deep some of the holes were because water from the recent rains filled them. He continued down the path between thick bushes and trees until he finally spotted Harry on the porch, slowly rocking.

Clay backed the truck near a huge oak tree that was so old its branches extended across the house, providing an umbrella of shade. Although Willow Mae despaired that lightning was going to strike that tree one day and it would crush the house, the oak had survived many years of hurricanes, storms, and floods. Clay suspected that when all else had changed on this island, that tree would still survive.

He cut the motor and opened the door. "When you going to fix that blasted road?" he said to Harry.

"When I get good and ready to, that's when." The chair squeaked as Harry stopped rocking and came out the seat.

Clay glared at his older brother. It wasn't like he had a nine-to-five job to go to daily. It shouldn't take much to at least keep the road drivable. Ryan had been making repairs around the place, all that he could find time for in his busy work schedule. "That road isn't decent enough to drive a tank through. I don't know how Willow Mae makes it with her car."

"She gets through just fine. Don't you be worrying yourself about it. Tend to your own business."

"Don't have time to with tending to yours. Come on over here and help me unload these supplies."

"If you had a told me you were going to town, I would have gone with you."

Clay seized two pairs of gloves from behind the seat and threw one pair to Harry. "Pauline went with me."

"How she doing?"

"Enjoying that baby of Delcia's."

Harry shook his head. "When you going to come to your senses and make things right with that girl of yours?"

Clay stopped and glared at Harry. "Take your own advice and mind your own business." He unlatched the tailgate to the truck and eased it down.

"Just ain't right, you treating her that way. She's always done right by you. Always been good. She makes one little slip up and you acting crazy."

Clay hefted himself up into the truck bed and grabbed a pack of shingles, ignoring his brother.

Harry plunked his hands on his hips and leaned toward Clay. "Like she don't have enough stress right now. She and Ryan's doing the job of three people."

Clay'd had enough and imitated Harry's pose, stooping over his brother. They were almost nose to nose. "You know, you were always a good one to be getting in everybody's business and dispensing advice. Why don't you take your own advice and keep things right with Willow Mae. She's a good woman. Much too good for the likes of you."

"Clay? That you?"

Clay turned toward the house. Willow Mae was leaning out the screen door peering toward the truck. She wasn't wearing her glasses and Clay knew she couldn't see three yards without them.

"Yeah, it's me." As much as Willow Mae and Harry argued, Willow Mae was always there to protect Harry when things got heated between the brothers.

"I thought I heard your voice."

Clay relaxed his stance and climbed off the truck bed. He loped toward the porch and climbed the steps. "How you doing, Willow Mae?"

"Okay for an old woman."

"Oh, posh. You still young and pretty."

Willow Mae laughed and hit him on the shoulder. "You always was the devil," she said before she grabbed him in a hug. "How's Pauline? I've got to stop by Delcia's to see her."

"She's looking forward to seeing you."

"Can you come to dinner tonight? I'd love to have you."

"I'll have her call you."

"Why don't I just call her now. Then I'll bring you out something to drink."

"You do that."

Clay returned to the truck to help unload the supplies in uneasy silence. Harry had no idea the worries that plagued him were about Delcia—and Ryan too. Ryan was engaged to marry the wrong woman and Delcia had ruined her life.

Delcia and Ranetta had breakfast together the next morning. Delcia had given Ranetta her own spoon. But before it was all over, Delcia needed a shower to get the oatmeal that Ranetta had scattered off of her. She left Ranetta at the kitchen table, more playing with than eating her oatmeal. The cereal was all over her face. Even with the bib, her clothing needed changing. But Delcia treasured these few moments with her child. "You're a mess." Delcia kissed her nose and Ranetta grinned up at her.

Her mother read the newspaper over a cup of coffee.

"I'll clean this up when I get back," Delcia said to her mother.

Pauline folded the paper and put it on the table. "Don't even think about it. Ranetta will want to play a while longer then I'll clean her up. You're not ready yet, are you sweetheart?" Pauline took the plastic cup with the spout that Delcia had filled with apple juice and handed it to Ranetta. The baby latched onto it and drank deeply.

Smiling, Delcia left to take a shower. Her humor left when she considered the shock on Carter's face when he had seen Ranetta yesterday. His reaction puzzled her. It wasn't that he wasn't mannerly; he had held the door for Jenny. But he'd seemed so surprised. Why? "Delcia," she said to herself. "You're being silly. That man didn't give you a second thought. You're blowing this all out of proportion."

Delcia sighed. There was no discounting that special something about him that just called to her. She had been trying to evade those feelings, but it was almost the way it had been with Bruce; her skin prickled every time Carter came into the shop or whenever she saw him walking along the campground. He seemed so troubled. Sometimes she found herself wishing there was something she could do to ease his sorrow—a sorrow that was laced with anger. When he let his guard down— which wasn't often—she could see leashed anger he barely held in check. What was causing those gut-wrenching emotions?

Delcia finished her shower and dressed in black jeans. Instead of a cotton shirt, she opted for a mauve silk blouse for a change. She spritzed on her favorite perfume, looped a gold chain around her neck, inserted earrings in her earlobes, and went into the kitchen. She wouldn't acknowledge that she'd dressed more carefully because of her attraction to Carter.

Her mother had wiped most of the cereal off Ranetta. Delcia kissed Ranetta on the cheek. "See you this evening, you two."

"Don't you look pretty," her mother said.

Delcia picked up her cup of coffee. "Why thank you. See you later." Delcia locked the kitchen door behind her as she made her way to the car. They had a busy day ahead of them. College kids were checking into the campground. They were fresh out of school for the summer and were wild and ready for freedom from exams. They liked to camp out for a week or two before they left for home.

Delcia drove the short distance to the camp store. It was seven-thirty and the store was already bursting with early morning shoppers. Like a homing pigeon, she focused on Carter. Quickly she stifled the awareness racing through her. No more camp flings for her. Once was enough to last a lifetime. Still, she thought, a woman would have to be blind not to notice his tall, muscular and graceful form. His brown complexion and startling eyes captured her the first time she had laid eyes on him. He gave a strong impression of strength in both character and build. But she also knew you couldn't tell a package by its wrapping. She knew nothing about this man and her fanciful impressions could lead her straight to trouble—trouble she wasn't prepared for. The kind of trouble she'd landed in once before—but never again.

Carter glanced up from his kitchen sink and saw Delcia walking along the water. He stuffed the sandwich meat back into the fridge, slipped on his shoes and ran after her.

"Mind if I join you?" he yelled out.

She turned at his voice and smiled. "Not at all,"

she said and waited for him to catch up. "Are you enjoying your stay with us?"

They strolled sided by side, enjoying the calm waves and the hint of a breeze.

"Very much, although I'm not here simply vacationing."

She raised her perfectly arched eyebrows. "Oh?"

He then revealed his identity and his relationship to David.

Delcia was hopping mad at the news.

Her lips tightened and she regarded Carter cautiously and suspiciously. Her hands bunched at her side. "I don't know what you plan to accomplish by coming here," she said through clenched teeth. "I'm deeply sorry for your loss and for Ranetta's, but I obviously didn't know Richard as well as I thought I did. Given his duplicity, I don't think I want to know him any better. I would appreciate medical information—for Ranetta's benefit."

"David was adopted. I can get information on him but not on his parents. We only know that his mother died in childbirth."

"What about her parents?"

"Unknown. We always assumed that she ran away from home after she got pregnant and used a false name."

"That's so sad." She wiped a weary hand across her forehead as they walked along the water's edge. Her heart went out to the young woman forced to run away from home, leaving the protection and comfort of her family when she found herself pregnant—an occasion that could be frightening and emotionally traumatic for a single woman. Delcia had been thirty-two and self-supporting when she discovered she was pregnant, but her independence couldn't stymie the emotional skirmish.

"What do you want from me?"

"I need to know what was going on the last few months of David's life. I'm looking for the person who murdered him."

"Murdered!" Delcia stopped. The statement sent a shudder through her. A couple of times when she and Richard were out, she got the sensation that they were being watched, but she put it down to paranoia. What had Richard been mixed up in? "Who would want him dead?"

"I don't know, but I don't believe in coincidences. Just think about it. Who would hunt on land that was clearly marked? Everyone in the area was aware of what the land was used for. Every few yards along the perimeter signs clearly state that no hunting was allowed. Also, that area is fenced off. Not that anyone can't cross the barrier, but they would have had to do so deliberately."

Delcia closed her eyes, then opened them, peering into the blue-gray waters that were as turbulent as Carter's eyes. "Oh, my God," she whispered.

Gliding a hand in his jeans pocket, Carter glanced toward his feet, then focused on Delcia as she absorbed the information. She was a beautiful woman, he thought, as a light-headed sensation brushed over him.

"All I know is that he was in Africa for the last year," she finally said.

Carter nodded. "David has never been out of the country."

Delcia threw up her hands. "Well, what's one more lie among many?"

"What was he supposedly doing in Africa?"

"He was searching for rare plant life that could be used for medicines. With the Congo devastated by war, he thought some plant life could be lost forever."

"Why would he go into a war area?"

"I don't know. Plant life is his field of expertise."

"David was a doctor."

"I know that. He has a doctorate in biology."

"A pediatrician." Frustrated, Carter rubbed the back of his neck. "You're not talking about the David I knew."

"As I told you, when he first came here he used the name Richard Connoly. It seems I didn't know him very well either."

"So when did the name David come into play?"

"When he checked into my campground as part of a bachelor party weekend. He and some friends of his stayed here for a couple of nights for fishing then left Friday morning. I confronted him before he left."

Well, he certainly wasn't a twin. Even adopted children had twins marked on the certificate and the foster care system always tried to keep siblings together. So where did this leave them—a split personality?

"When did you first meet David?"

Delcia sighed. "Thanksgiving year before last. As I said, he'd used the name Richard then. He stayed for the holiday, then came back after Christmas. He rented a cabin. Look, I don't know your purpose. I haven't asked for anything from his family. I wish you luck in your search."

"I saw your baby yesterday."

Delcia tensed, remembering the odd expression on his face. "I know that."

"She has David's eyes."

Delcia nodded. "Yes, she does."

"I need to know what was going on with David so that I can . . ." he shrugged his shoulders and glanced away, "make some sense out of what has happened."

"I only knew him here and whatever he told me—which is obviously lies. I don't know anything about his life away from the campground."

"How long did he visit the campground last year?"

"For a month. He left for Africa the first week in February. I didn't see or hear from him since—until the week of the bachelor party."

Carter pulled the coin from under his T-shirt. "One more question. David wore a chain around his neck like this."

Delcia shook her head. "He never wore a chain like that here."

"Are you certain?"

Delcia nodded. "Very. I would have remembered." She turned toward the office. "I have to get back to work." She left him with compound emotions. It was evident that the loss of his foster brother was a painful experience. They must have grown close through the years. She thought of Ryan. She wouldn't even go there.

Delcia was also angry, though she couldn't cast her anger on Carter. David had wronged her, not Carter. But his pain pulled at her. He grew up without the security of family that she'd been raised with and his brother must have meant an awful lot to him.

She couldn't imagine life without her family. Uncle Harry and her dad were always fighting about something, at family gatherings on Thanksgiving, Christmas and at reunions—but they were brothers.

Delcia wondered if Carter had any family left—other foster brothers. Richard had told her that he was an only child. He never mentioned brothers or even that he was a foster child.

"Murder," she whispered. Fear ripped through her. Would his murder affect Ranetta? Could whoever murdered David or Richard come after her baby? She turned and started to approach Carter. With his hands in his pockets, he gazed at the ocean. She'd leave him in peace for now and ask Jenny to keep a closer eye on Ranetta.

Carter now had an excuse to call Louise. He dialed her number as soon as he returned to the RV.

"Carter," she demanded in a stringent voice. "How long is it going to take you to probate David's estate. I don't know why you're dawdling."

"These things take time, Louise. I'll complete it as soon as possible."

"See that you do. We have bills to pay and only two thirds of our regular income. We have to pay a temporary pediatrician to take David's place. It's really put us in a bind."

"Nice to see you recovered so well, Louise," he marked sarcastically.

"I'm doing the best that I can," she snapped.

"Life must go on, after all. We have a business to maintain."

"I called to ask you about David. Were there any concerns with him in the last year?"

"Of course not. David was one of the most reliable men I've ever met."

"Could you tell me where he was the last week in January last year?"

"How am I to know where he was a year ago?" Carter heard her sigh over the line. "More than likely he was here. He never took very much time off."

"Would you check his calendar to be sure?"

"Yes, Carter, I will. Although I don't see what that has to do with his estate."

"It's always a pleasure, Louise." Carter hung up. It was always a trial holding a conversation with that woman. Carter could well understand how David would prefer Delcia's warmth to the reptilian Louise.

He and David had never been attracted to the same women. And now suddenly—Delcia. The concept didn't bear thought.

Carter rubbed his hand over his head. He never ran from the truth whether he liked it or not. Reality always had a way of staring him in the face. He was a realist. He was attracted to his brother's—what? The woman he had an affair with?—a baby by?

"Delcia . . . Delcia. What is wrong with you?"

Delcia glanced at Wanda who had her hands on her hips. "What's wrong?"

"I'm asking you that. You've been somewhere else since I got here."

Delcia shook her head. "It's nothing. Just thinking about work."

"That's nothing new. You've never gotten this preoccupied about work before."

"Not a good day for me, that's all."

"Girl, you've been through so much lately. You just need some time to catch your breath."

"That must be it." Delcia stacked the last plate in the dishwasher and closed the door.

Wanda wiped the stove, rinsed the dishcloth out, hung it over the water spout, and regarded her friend. "It's more than that, isn't it?"

Delcia glanced at the woman who'd been her friend for what seemed forever. "Let me peek at Ranetta. Take your lemonade out back and I'll meet you there."

"I'll refill your glass."

Delcia went into the baby's room and tucked the sheet around her. Then she turned on the baby monitor and carried the receiver with her.

Closing the screen door behind her, she looked towards the sky. There was a nice breeze tonight and the stars were shining brightly. They looked at peace millions of miles away. It was amazing that more than a hundred years had passed since their light started its journey to earth.

She set the monitor on the table between two cushioned wicker lounge chairs.

"One of the guests who checked into the campground is Richard's brother. He believes that Richard was murdered."

"Given his duplicity, that can't come as a shock."

"The paper said it was an accident."

"Who knows who he's been playing fast and loose with. Delcia," she said cautiously. "You really didn't know him."

"But murder?"

"You think everyone is as kindhearted as you are. Still, he seemed so nice last spring."

"Don't let the looks fool you."

"Is he as handsome as Richard?"

"They look nothing alike. They were foster brothers."

Wanda took a sip of her drink. "Have you told Ryan? Or your parents?"

"Not yet. Ryan's so protective. I don't want him fighting my battles. He has enough on his mind with LaToya."

"That's what he gets for dating an outsider. He should have chosen an island girl."

"There's no accounting for taste. I don't know what he sees in her. She's going to make him miserable."

Wanda regarded her. "But you won't tell him that."

"No, I won't. I can't choose a wife for him."

"What are you going to do about Richard's brother?"

"There's nothing I can do about him. Still, Richard was Ranetta's father so I feel I should be doing something."

"The way he two-timed you? You don't owe him a thing."

Delcia shook her head. "I owe it to Ranetta."

Wanda smiled. "She's such a precious baby. And to think after all these years."

Delcia heard a car door slam and a minute later her parents entered through the screen door.

"Pauline, you got anything for indigestion," Clay Anderson asked. "You'd think Willow Mae would know how to bake food by now. Those pork chops were loaded with fat."

They were in the family room by now and Delcia watched her mom, Pauline, fish in her purse for the Tums and handed two to Clay. "You ate three helpings."

"Anything with that much grease got to be good," he said and disappeared into the kitchen.

Pauline sighed and strolled onto the deck.

"How was dinner?" Delcia asked her mother.

"The meal was delicious. The conversation was a bit awkward," her mother said.

Delcia didn't need to ask if her dad and Uncle Harry were fighting again. Their arguments were a family trademark.

"Well, dear, we're going to bed. Good night."

"See you tomorrow."

Silence reigned for moments. Only the sound of crashing waves and crickets permeated the night.

"Do you know what's really crazy?" Delcia finally asked Wanda.

"What."

"I feel . . . these vibes . . . this attraction to Carter, of all men. Richard and I were just friends. I never felt this magic. Do you know what I mean?"

"Oh, no!" Wanda groaned.

"I haven't told another soul, but it's there and strong. You know, like what I felt for Bruce in high school, yet different, somehow."

"What are you going to do about it?"

Delcia thought for a moment. "Nothing. I'm sure it'll pass."

"Did your attraction for Bruce pass?"

Delcia shook her head. "You know it didn't." What she'd felt for Bruce had only grown stronger.

Four

Pauline dropped her purse on the bed in the guest room and planted her hands on her hips, the very pose she'd used with recalcitrant students as a teacher or with Delcia and Ryan when they were growing up. Right now she had that stubborn look that Clay was quite familiar with when her anger flared.

"This has gone on long enough," she snapped. "You're fighting with everybody. I thought we were in a war zone instead of dinner at Willow Mae and Harry's with you two men going at each other back and forth like snapping turtles. What is going on with you?"

Clay stomped to the stuffed chair and dropped into the blue cushions. He pulled off his shoes, one by one as if the weight of the world rested on his shoulders.

"I'm waiting," she demanded. Pauline had never been a demanding woman, but when she got her dander up there was no getting around her. She was like a cool breeze that kept everything on its course; on a particularly hot day, one didn't recognize that it was there, until it stopped.

He looked up at his wife and shrugged. "I don't know."

Pauline sighed. "You know what's eating at you? It's this rift between you and Delcia. She's always been the apple of your eye. If you don't make up with her, it's going to take you to an early grave. She doesn't deserve this silent treatment from you. You know you love her."

"Of course I love her," he roared as if he'd fight anyone who said otherwise.

"Hush. You'll wake the baby."

Clay swiped his hand across his face in a weary gesture and hopped out of the seat, pacing the length of the blue room only to stop by the window that looked off onto the ocean he both loved and hated. As sweet as she could be one day, the next, her fierce winds and crushing waves could snap a proud structure in two. But right now he couldn't see it; he could only hear the waves crashing against the shore. He peered out into the dark cloud-shrouded night, deep into thoughts that had tormented his soul for a year and a half.

"That's just it. Pauline, I love her so much that her treachery still cuts me as sharply as if she'd stabbed me with a knife."

"Honey, she wasn't trying to hurt you."

"I know that." He turned from the window to face his wife. "Raising a child alone isn't the kind of life I wanted for her." He dug his hands into his pockets. "Hell, when I was growing up, my sisters had to marry the men they left the house with on simple dates. But did I make life that difficult for Delcia? No. I've always trusted her."

"It's not the life I would have chosen for her either, but people make mistakes. Even our children.

We have to live with what is, not with what we want the situation to be."

"Mistakes?" he said, marching to the bed. "You don't think she knew what she was doing when she went to bed with that . . . that . . ." He sat beside Pauline, his forearms on his legs. "She didn't know anything about him. Didn't know his family. Just because the world has gone loose doesn't mean that I have to accept that for my family."

Pauline placed her hand on his arm and stroked him. "Clay," she said quietly. "you're being too hard on her. I understand that we were raised in a different time and we both came from strong, upstanding, strict families and we wanted our children to adhere to the family's code. But she's still our daughter."

"She knew better." He shook his head. "Now-a-days kids talk back to their parents and act just like the parent was the child. More and more young boys choose the wrong path because they don't listen to their elders. When I'm talking to my friends I always shake my head, smug in my belief that the parents had been too lenient on their children. And with the government sticking its nose where it has no business, making it hard to parent children. How many parents have we heard lamenting that the kids came home from school telling them that they can get them thrown into jail for chastising them. Can you believe that? We're not talking about abuse, because they still escape the system. They're just making it difficult for parents who're trying to raise their kids right. They'd just have to carry me on to jail. We haven't been lenient on Delcia or Ryan." Clay sighed. "They've been good kids, haven't they?"

Pauline nodded.

"Took the straight and narrow road until Delcia slipped up. And now Delcia's got to go it alone. She's got no husband to stand with her when the going gets tough. And it will. It always does." Anguish clouded his senses. "She's acting like a sixteen-year-old instead of a woman who's thirty-three."

"Then we'll help her. Ryan will help her. And she's strong enough to handle whatever life throws her—to do what she will need to do to raise her daughter in the proper way."

"Pauline," he said with a croak in his voice. "I just wonder sometimes if Delcia and I will ever find our way back to the warm relationship we once had. I've missed her terribly."

Soft, warm eyes regarded him while soft hands stroked him. "Why don't you make the first move? If you just meet her part of the way . . ." Then Pauline uttered the words she knew would pull at his heartstrings. "She loves you, you know. You're so much alike."

Clay, however, felt he was right. "It's not that she did wrong that makes me so angry, because I love my granddaughter. Until she came along, I'd forgotten just how precious they are and I started to remember Delcia and Ryan when they were growing up. I wouldn't ask anything for Ranetta except a father to help guide her in the right way—a father to protect her—to teach her right from wrong—to love her."

"Honey . . ."

"I know that women marry two and three times in these modern days. But I don't want that for Delcia." He took his weathered hand and caressed Pauline's soft, dark skin.

"I love you more now than the day I married you. You've given me so many precious years," he whispered. "You've given me two wonderful children. You're truly my soul mate." He watched tears gather in Pauline's eyes and spill on her cheeks. He lifted his hand and wiped them away with his thumb and took her hand in his. "I've never regretted one day of our thirty-five years together. But I want that kind of love for Delcia and Ryan. I want Delcia's husband to love all my grandkids the way he would love the children of his own flesh and blood. And not all men can do that. And if he didn't love Ranetta just that much, Delcia would never marry him. Now, that much I know. I want my daughter to have a full and complete life—as full and as satisfying as my life has been with you."

Pauline wrapped her arms around Clay, leaned her head against his strong shoulder. She closed her eyes and sighed. "Oh, Clay, my love. You need to tell her this." She lifted her head to look him in the eyes. "Let her know how you feel. She thinks you won't forgive her for going against your strict moral code." Pauline leaned back and tapped his chest with her hand. "She doesn't really know what's here. And only you can tell her that."

Clay nodded, stroking the dark strands of Pauline's soft unbound hair.

"Clay," Pauline whispered, stroking his chest, his shoulders. "I love you." Her hand inched beneath his shirt to tangle in his gray chest hairs and sluggishly descended to the belt buckle.

Clay sucked in a breath and caught her face between his hands, feeling himself harden as readily as he had on their wedding night. He looked lovingly into her face, caressed the soft wrinkled skin with the back of his hands. After all these years, she knew just where to touch him to stir his blood to boiling. Loving Pauline was like the very air he breathed—necessary and so much a part of him. She'd always made him feel ten feet tall. He'd go to his grave loving this woman who looked at him with a coaxing, beguiling smile.

Gradually, he lowered his head toward hers and kissed her lips—lips that immediately softened beneath his own.

The next day turned out hot and muggy. Carter strolled past a row of cabins.

"Darn it," he heard and swung around to see what was the matter.

Ryan was struggling with a cabin door.

The man glared at the door, then dropped the hammer into his tool belt and positioned the door in line with the hinges. Holding it in place, he put the bolt in place and retrieved the hammer. Before he could knock the bolt in position, it dropped to the porch.

The air turned ripe with curses.

"Need some help with that?" Carter asked, changing directions.

Irritated, Ryan glanced up and blew out a long breath. "Sure. One of our guests left the door open during the storm and the wind tore it off the hinges. I've been working with this thing . . ." He tightened his mouth in frustration.

Carter neared the door. "I'll hold it in place while you pound the bolt in."

In no time, the bolts were hammered in place.

Ryan straightened and blew out a long breath, putting the tools into the toolbox.

Carter took a peek inside. The log structure consisted of two rooms. A queen-sized bed lay against the wall in one room and twin beds occupied the second room. Missing was a bathroom.

"Thanks, man. I've been struggling with that for a while." Ryan took the cap off his head and wiped his forehead with his arm. "Have you been fishing yet?"

"Not yet."

"Besides our fishing crowd, some of our guests like to just rest or take in the scenery and the camp activities that start up this Friday. Others find the water's too turbulent for boating or fishing."

"I've done my share of fishing with my father and brother," Carter said. "Seems odd somehow to go fishing without them."

"Will they be joining you here?"

Carter shook his head. "No." He wondered if Delcia had mentioned who he really was, but then guessed that she hadn't. Ryan wouldn't be so friendly if he knew that Carter's brother was her baby's father. Perhaps he could use her silence as an opportunity to get closer with her family. "Actually, I just retired from the navy."

Ryan laughed. "Well, then. Rough water's nothing for you."

"I spent my share of the last twenty years on ships, that's for sure," Carter agreed. "I was thinking of opening a campground in Virginia."

"What part?"

"Something right off ninety-five—on a river. A

good stopover for travelers going farther South. Near a good fishing spot I think. I've looked at a couple of spots."

"Have you ever worked at a campground?"

"Nope. But I've done plenty of sleeping rough in the navy."

"I bet you did."

"I'm available if you need any help. I'd welcome it in exchange for training. Give me firsthand knowledge on how to run a campground."

"I'll take you up on that. We're pretty short handed right now."

Carter started toward his RV.

"We'll see you tomorrow if you want to start that soon."

Carter turned. "I'll be there."

LaToya, one of the most startlingly beautiful women Carter had ever laid eyes on, sat beside Ryan's mother, Mrs. Anderson, looking bored and restless. And what was more, the woman knew she was drop-dead gorgeous. She crossed her tight jeans-clad legs and twisted at an angle to give a peek at her well-shaped behind.

Carter had learned that she wanted Ryan to leave the campground to work at an accounting firm in Triangle Park.

The park didn't stand a chance. This woman knew how to ply her wiles on a man. Ryan was a done deal; it was only a matter of when. But talking with the man over the last few days, Carter realized that Ryan really loved working at the park, and he was torn between lust and family responsibility. Good luck, Carter thought, because LaToya almost had Ryan in her clutches and once she got him, she wasn't going to let go.

"You put in a good day's work," Clay said, tearing Carter from his musings. He surrounded the cone-shaped stack of wood with twigs and branches that had fallen as a result of the storm. In a few minutes they'd light it and make a huge bonfire where the campground's patrons would roast hot dogs and marshmallows.

Carter merely nodded and added his armful of wood to the structure. The park brought in a few cords of wood every fall for the winter season. The night was cool enough for one last fire.

Clay had grilled him for the last two days on his background and Carter had answered in short statements, sticking as close to the truth as possible. But they'd barely had a quiet minute, what with hammering boards in place on the picnic tables and the other work. Carter had wondered how long the silence would last.

"Should be a good crowd," Carter said.

Clay glanced at the children who watched from afar, eager to approach the structure. Some of the fishermen had brought their families with them. A group of children playing around the edge of the lawn were so thrilled about the bonfire they could barely contain their excitement. College students sat on camp chairs or on the ground, crossing their legs Indian-style.

Finally, Clay took a lighter out of his pocket. He lit a cone of rolled up paper and used it to light the kindling. Carter repeated the procedure on the opposite side of the stack.

As they nursed the flame to life, families drew closer to the blaze. Families, Carter thought as he glanced at Mrs. Anderson, who held Ranetta. Ranetta was immersed in love and security.

"Here are the hot dogs!" Delcia carried a pan brimming with them. Barbara walked behind her with a tray of buns. Carter shook his head and took the pan from Delcia, setting it on the table.

"Thanks. I'll get the sticks and condiments, and . . ." The rest of her sentence fizzled as she turned and left. She was obviously still uncertain about him working at the campground, and as Carter watched her lush backside as she walked toward the store, he couldn't tell if he was here because of Ranetta, or his brother, or because of the traitorous, magnetic attraction he felt for Delcia.

Carter watched her long strides and was appalled at the feelings that pulled at his gut.

Perhaps working with Clay and Ryan the last couple of days was altering his perception of all of them. She seemed more real—more likable—less likely to have committed a crime. He was letting his feelings for this family intrude on his search for justice. And if she wasn't involved, where did he go from here?

Mark came over to where he stood. He was Delcia's cousin by her Uncle Spike who had died a few years back. "Reminds me of my football days," he said. "We had a bonfire every fall."

Carter had learned early on that Mark used any excuse to take a break. He'd also added on a few pounds since those days, Carter had heard—quite a few.

"Never had bonfires at my high school."

"Ah, man. The cheerleaders were what they were all about."

Carter chuckled. "I'm going to help Delcia bring out the food. Come on."

As they climbed the wooden porch to the store, they passed a wood carver sitting in the corner, whittling a chunk of wood into a duck decoy. A couple of old men had pulled up rockers near him and they watched the goings-on and lamented about the passing of the old days.

As Carter entered the building, he knew very well that Delcia wouldn't appreciate his presence. He had a sneaking suspicion that she was bothered by her attraction to him more than anything else. He smiled at that.

It was just too darn bad, because he was here to stay awhile.

Two hours later, Carter watched Delcia playing with her baby. Ranetta was wide awake, entranced by the flames from the bonfire. Pauline assured everyone that the baby would sleep soundly after hours of fresh air. Carter realized that it also gave Delcia a chance to spend time with her child.

He knew very little about children—especially ones so tiny—and wondered how old Ranetta was. Delcia tickled her tummy with her face and the child fell into a fit of giggles while pulling Delcia's hair. Delcia emitted a tiny squeal and untangled tiny fingers from the dark strands. The simple interaction stirred something deep and dormant in Carter.

Had anyone loved him that much when he was a child? The last two days were the first time in a long time he'd thought about babies and reflected on his own formative years. Had he been placed with foster parents who were tender and kind to him? Did they rock him when he had trouble falling asleep while teething or during a fretful night after an immunization shot? From the time that he could remember, the foster parents he had were not unkind to him, they just never wanted to keep him.

"Clay says you're been such a great help to them and that you want to open your own campground."

Carter glanced to his right and realized Pauline had sat down beside him. He didn't often relax enough for someone to sneak up on him. There was something warm and comforting about Pauline that pulled out the best in people. "I was thinking a small one between Richmond and Emporia. I saw a For Sale sign for some property that joins the Nottoway River. Be good for fishing in that area. During the summers, the hotels fill up quickly. A few cabins would work for the one nighters who stop on their way further south."

"You couldn't find better teachers than my children." The statement was laced with unmistakable pride. "Years ago, Clay and his brother, Spike, owned this land." She shifted positions in her seat. "Some of Spike's fishing buddies brought camping gear and went fishing a couple of weeks each year. It wasn't long before it created a ripple effect. His friends brought their friends and the crowds grew larger and larger each year until Spike and Clay built this small shack with a rest room and a cold shower." She laughed a delicate musical sound. This woman was all grace and elegance. "Let me tell you, there were long lines for those meager facilities, but Delcia saw an opportunity, and from the time she was ten, she would regale us with tales of how she'd operate her own campground. Spike would laugh at her tales, but when he passed away he left his share of the land to Delcia. And when Clay retired, he'd lived through so many island storms that he didn't want to retire here. He loves visiting the area, but he no longer wants to make repairs or live with the worry."

She gazed at the people milling around and a softness came to her eyes. "This island is a special place with a rhythm of its own. Clay was principal of the elementary school until he retired, and I taught in that school. We taught because we didn't want to leave this place. If Delcia hadn't started this campground, I think she would have taught too, just to stay on this island."

Carter was thoroughly engrossed in the tale. "When she graduated from high school she started her campground?"

Mrs. Anderson shook her head. "It wasn't quite that easy. She wanted her college degree. So her father told her if she got it, he'd deed the rest of the land to Ryan and her. Delcia got into a high school college-partnership program. In her senior year, she took several college courses. Then she attended every summer to finish up in three years. With degree in hand, she approached Clay and he handed her the deed to the land." Suddenly sadness swamped her. "Then she married Bruce and convinced him that he'd enjoy owning a campground much more than working in construction."

Carter could imagine that it took little to convince a man in love—especially by someone with a body and face like Delcia's.

"The three of them, Delcia, Ryan, and Bruce, built all of this with their own hands. Delcia nailed shingles on roofs and hammered two-by-fours just like the boys."

Carter imagined Delcia on a roof hammering nails with her derriere pointed at Bruce and smiled. He guessed there was a lot of starch beneath that sweet face. And if Bruce was behind her, well he'd follow her around all day.

"As they say, the rest is history. They started out very primitive."

"I thought primitive was the goal of camping. Getting back to nature and all that."

"To a certain extent. If that were the case you wouldn't be living in a mobile home with all the modern conveniences. People still like hot showers and clean rest rooms. Look around," she said.

Carter did. He saw families and friends, some singing camp songs, other conversing. Children were playing, teenagers, chattering and courting. He saw comfort, camaraderie, love.

"They've made this into more of a family retreat. The fishing conventions used to draw only men who loved to fish and a few wives, daughters, and sons who loved the sport. Now it's a family affair. Families love planned activities like this bonfire and hot dog roast. Add to that all the lasting friendships that have been formed here. Campers look forward to getting together once or twice a year. Most of the people you see here return year after year. The word spreads and business grows."

Carter hated lying to this nice lady. While he enjoyed working here, his main purpose wasn't to open a campground and the deceit nagged at his conscience.

Carter glanced around at the crowd still milling around the flames that were slowly dying. Another hour or two, he thought, before the fire flickers out completely.

"So, how did you hear about this campground?"

"A buddy of mine from Raleigh mentioned it. Some friends of his camp here." Time to get the conversation from him. "How far away did you and Clay move?"

"We live in Ashville."

"Mountain country."

"We like it. I could do without so much snow."

"My, ah . . . my . . . well . . ." He cleared his throat. "The woman who took care of me hated the snow, too." He didn't know why he mentioned Nadine. He'd always called her by her last name. Somehow she was never his mom. The words just wouldn't come. He could see in her eyes that she wished he would call her Mom. He glanced at Pauline out of the corner of his eye. She reminded him of Nadine.

Mrs. Anderson gazed at him questionably for a moment. "Well, you've been a tremendous help to my family. I'm grateful."

"I'm learning a lot."

"So when do you plan to open your park?"

"I'm not sure yet. It'll be at least another summer. I want to learn as much as I can about this business before I take it on. So many businesses go under."

She laughed. "You don't strike me as the cautious type. Now, Delcia," she glanced at her daughter fondly, "once she makes up her mind, there's no stopping her."

As Ryan locked the door to the store, Delcia puzzled over Carter. She still hadn't told her family that he was David's foster brother. "I don't know if it was a good idea hiring someone we don't know, Ryan. Even if he is a help to us," she said as Ryan pocketed the key.

"He gave me a list of references. One was from someone who owns a security firm near Ashville. Believe me, I called and they gave him exemplary references. Now you can sleep at night, knowing that he isn't a serial killer in our midst."

"I guess a week or two won't hurt."

They started toward their cars. Delcia lived two miles from the park; Ryan another half mile from her.

"I was thinking more of the entire summer. He could be a help to us. Most of the summer employees are students who can't be left alone. An adult who's training for his own business would be more responsible. He's been great so far. You'll have more time for Ranetta."

And it will give Ryan time to get away with LaToya, Delcia realized. He needed time to develop their relationship and see what else was out there. He needed to get a feel for the corporate world to see if that was really where he would fit in. She wondered if he only got into this business because he was following in her footsteps. He deserved his freedom, if that was what he wanted. Though she didn't want a relative of David's working at her campground—she realized she couldn't turn away the extra help.

"I'm sure he'll work out just fine," she finally said, resigned to dealing with Carter's alluring presence.

Ryan threw his arm around her shoulder as they walked to the car. "I've been feeling a little punchy lately."

"I know."

"You need a break, too. Working at full speed for three years has taken its toll. Plus, you worked extra while I finished up my degree. I really appreciate that."

"I was more than pleased to do it. Your accounting skills have been a great asset to the park." Then she thought, did he feel he must stay because of her? "Ryan, you don't feel you have to stay because of the time you took away for your studies, do you?"

"No. And stop second guessing every statement I make. I'll make my decision based on what I want for my future. If I do decide to go, it won't be before September and not before I've trained someone to take over my responsibilities."

He wasn't going to find anyone who would work the hours he worked and they both knew it. They would have to hire at least two people.

"If Carter likes it here well enough," Ryan continued, "he may decide to stay on."

Delcia didn't comment on that statement. They reached their cars. "LaToya's waiting at your house?"

Ryan sighed. "Yeah." She'd left in a huff hours ago, angry that he couldn't take more time off to spend with her. He watched Delcia drive away and waved to the night security man who rounded the corner. Then he entered his own car and drove toward home to another argument.

He drove slowly toward the house that he grew up in. When his parents left, he'd bought the house from them. Houses were a great deal cheaper then. At that time, the real estate prices were still reasonable in this area. The value of property on other islands had soared, but not on Coree. But now that had changed since there was practically nothing for sale here. With the campground, more and more people saw the value of the island. Even though they were plagued with storms, a full-blown hurricane hadn't hit the island since the early nineteen hundreds, and this gave people a false sense of security. He and Delcia had been offered a fortune for their land, but they were not willing to sell. He couldn't imagine a better life.

Delcia drove into her driveway and Ryan cruised by. Both their homes faced the ocean. Ryan turned into his driveway. LaToya had left the porch light on. It was time to face the music.

LaToya met him at the door in a virginal white nightgown with thin spaghetti shoulder straps. The contrast of the white gown against her beautiful dark skin was entrancing. However, LaToya was no virgin—she was wild and sexy and she knew just how to please him.

The fatigue instantly fell from Ryan as she wrapped her arms around him. She was sweet-smelling and bewitching. This was a reception worthy of a king.

"I've been waiting for you." Her sultry whisper caressed his ear. He enclosed her within his embrace, holding her tight against his body. The thin wisp of fabric she wore concealed nothing. This would be a night to remember after all, he thought as he pressed his face to her neck and inhaled deeply.

Fleetingly, he wondered if this was the prelude to a long, lasting relationship or if it was pure lust and sex. He darted kisses on her neck, her breasts, as she groaned.

At this moment, he really didn't care.

Five

Carter took the eleven o'clock ferry to Morehead City and met Louise at a restaurant for lunch.

He found her pacing next to her car. He took a moment to study her as he parked his bike. The instant she recognized him, she turned up her nose at the bike and leather jacket. She probably had visions of him sprawled in a bar or riding with a gang from state to state.

Her scrutiny gave him equal time to take her measure. Louise was coldly resplendent in a navy suit and matching heels. Her hair was combed back and caught in a bun. It highlighted the delicate bone structure of her deceptive face. Louise wasn't demure or delicate—she was a human shark in expensive garb.

"Thank you for meeting with me," he said as they settled at their table. "Let me tell you again how sorry I am for your loss."

In an uncustomary move, Louise reached across the table and placed her hand on Carter's. "You and David were very close. Even though you and I never saw eye to eye, I'm aware that David's parting was as much of a loss for you, Carter, as it has been for me."

"Thank you, Louise."

She moved her hand away, wrapped her fingers around the water glass, and took a delicate sip. When the waiter arrived, they ordered their meal. Carter wasn't fooled one bit by her demeanor.

"In answer to your question about David's condition, he had a physical two months before he died," she began as they waited for their meal. "I talked to his doctor and he said David was in excellent physical and mental health. Dr. Albert Stover is his physician if you want to talk with him. Why did you want to know?"

"I've just had reports that he wasn't quite himself a few months before his death."

"From whom?"

"Friends," Carter replied.

"They don't know what they're talking about. David and I worked together closely. If something was wrong, believe me, I would have known. Let me assure you that David was a very healthy man in every way."

She glanced around the room. "I wish you had let me choose the restaurant. I find a wall hung with fishnets, life preservers and starfish very tacky. We have much nicer restaurants here."

Carter reflected on the items she hated but found he liked the informal seafood restaurant just fine. Moreover, this meeting was solely about David. Who cared about where they dined?

But then, Carter noticed the lack of an air of loss about Louise. He didn't expect her to languish in misery forever, but he couldn't help pondering how many tears she'd shed for her late fiancé.

"Did you check David's calendar regarding his whereabouts in January?"

She checked her watch. "David was in Las Vegas attending a medical conference."

"For how long?"

"One week," she said, sending him a quizzical look. She smiled at a couple who passed their table.

"What about the other three weeks?"

Her eyes swung to his. "He was home, of course."

Carter regarded her. He hoped his feelings about Louise weren't clouding his vision or making him think she was more guilty than she was.

After lunch, Carter drove to Greenville to Rice's trailer. The man had called earlier to tell him he'd completed the search.

Rice was waiting for him.

"I came up dry. A shooter wasn't hired within a hundred miles of this place."

Damn, Carter thought, as he paid the man the balance of his payment and left. Usually someone stumbled and bragged of their deed, which is how people like Rice stayed in business. Obviously, the shooter was the person who wanted David dead, Carter thought on his drive to the island. His mind immediately went to Louise, wondering if she'd donned men's clothing and tracked David in the forest.

Carter approached Delcia just after she closed the store. Ryan had spent the evening with LaToya, and Carter had worked with Delcia, but they'd had no time alone together. As he walked her to her car, he broached the subject of the luncheon he'd had and wondered if perhaps he was using this as an excuse to spend more time with her—time alone with no employees or campers around.

"I talked to Louise, today."

He looked down at her lush mouth and watched her reaction in the dim halogen light overhead.

"And what did she have to offer?" she asked.

He wondered what it would feel like to kiss her and something inside him tightened. "Not much. Nothing helpful, actually." He decided not to tell her that David was supposed to have been in Las Vegas. What good would it do?

"Your search seems to be going nowhere."

"Patience, my dear Watson," he said in a British accent.

That got a tired chuckle from her. "I'm not very patient."

Carter leaned against the car. She threw her purse inside and stood about a foot from him. They were insulated by trees. From their vantage point, they couldn't see any of the campers, but low whispers carried in the night air along with the sounds of crickets and the ocean tides.

The tides lulled Carter to sleep at night. He wondered if he'd miss them when he left and knew that he would. It was like singing a lullaby to a baby.

The waning aroma of Delcia's perfume teased his senses, even though they were a foot apart.

"What did you do in the navy?" she asked.

"I was a SEAL."

"Were you any good?"

"The best."

"I've never met a humble SEAL."

"A modest man wouldn't be a SEAL," he said with such assurance that Delcia chuckled again.

"Did you like being a SEAL?"

"It's more than an occupation. It's a way of life."

"Than it must have been difficult for you to leave."

Her comment reminded him of his purpose, and that he shouldn't be trying to put the make on David's woman, although she wasn't his woman any longer. Carter swiped a hand across his face. He didn't know what to think about David. He couldn't have been in two places at once.

Louise had no reason to lie, at least about that.

Ranetta's innocent green eyes didn't lie.

Delcia moved beside him and relaxed against the car. He realized they were assessing each other.

Because of their elite military position, many people feared the SEALs. They perceived them more as fighting machines than men. He wondered what Delcia thought about him. Whatever she felt, it wasn't fear.

He smiled. Her beauty and her spirit were as intoxicating as fine cognac.

Suddenly she stood and backed to the car door. "Well, I have to be going."

"See you tomorrow," he said.

She hurried into the car and started the motor. Carter waited until she pulled out of the parking slot before he started his slow trek to his campsite.

He hadn't thought seriously about a woman since he was engaged to Laurisa ten years ago. Her father had been an admiral and disapproved of his daughter's interest in Carter. They were stationed in Hawaii. The admiral had shipped her back to San Diego pronto and he had warned Carter to stay away from his daughter. After all, Carter had no family, no background, nothing to offer his daughter. Besides, he'd never let his daughter marry a SEAL.

Carter knew then that he was good enough to fight for his country, but not good enough to marry the daughter of the man who sent him on dangerous missions.

The warning hadn't deterred Carter. He searched for Laurisa and found her. But when he arrived on her doorstep, he discovered quickly that she wasn't willing to go against her father's wishes. There was nothing left for Carter to do but leave.

Carter was willing to bet that Delcia was made of sterner stuff.

After a shower, Carter drove to Wanda's. The quiet restaurant he'd visited before was a far cry from the bar he entered at 10:30 P.M. The loud music hit him even as he drove into the yard. The jukebox, a relic from the fifties, blasted out oldies.

In the dim interior light, the crowd seemed a mixture of tourists and locals. Carter glanced around the dark room and took a seat at the bar. He had just given his drink order when someone came up behind him.

"Hey, Carter."

Carter sighed. He just wanted to nurse his drink and drown his miseries this one night. He turned and greeted Randall.

"Didn't realize you were back."

"Pulled in an hour ago. Come on over and join us. Just a couple of my buddies."

The bartender put Carter's drink on the bar. Carter left money and carried his drink to Randall's table. He'd met the two men sitting there before—Eric and Mason. Eric had a creamed coffee complexion and Mason was dark.

"I was just telling Randy that we got a good chance of winning that race this year. Are you entering?"

The sailboat race was coming up on Sunday. "Hadn't planned on it," Carter said.

"We race every year. Been three years since we've won."

"I take it's a big event here."

"Hell, yeah. Folks come from all over." Eric sipped his bourbon and shook his head.

"Even from Canada," Mason offered.

"Seen you working at the park. They hire you on?"

"Just helping out a bit. Got nothing better to do for the summer," Carter said. "You guys from Morehead City?"

"Raleigh," Eric said.

"I live west of Morehead." Mason drank his beer.

"We can always use an extra hand," Randall said.

Carter shook his head. "I'll be working." Carter sampled his own drink. "You all spend a lot of time here. What do you do back home?"

"Do?" Eric asked and roared.

"Like in work," Carter said.

"Well, I run my old man's company—sometimes." Eric laughed.

Randall hooted. "Your old man don't let you near his company most times. He just want you out of his hair."

"It'll still be waiting for me."

"Now me," Mason said, "we own all this farmland

west of Morehead. I've got to work for my money. I can't spend days fishing the way these guys can."

"Give me a break," Randall said. "Your foreman sees to the farm."

"Yeah, but I've got to work right along with him every day. Farms are more modernized now."

"That's the darn truth," Randall said. "My wife's old man's got an investment in a farm. They aren't like they used to be. Everything's industrialized."

"Randy here's got the rich father-in-law and a psychiatrist for a wife," Eric offered.

"Maybe she needs to see one herself to tell her why she puts up with him," Mason said.

Randy cursed. "Screw you."

"She's going to stick a screw to you if you don't show up real soon. How long you been away?"

"Don't no woman tell me what to do. I'm the man in my house."

"Tell that garbage to somebody who don't know better," Eric sneered.

Carter grew bored of the argument. He saw Ryan come in and excused himself from the group and joined him at his table. He never had much patience with ne'er-do-wells. He wished they didn't feel they needed to include him in their little group.

And just maybe, he thought, they'd hit a little too close to home. He didn't know his father, but he imagined him to be a man who cared little about responsibilities—a man sitting around a bar like these men were, not caring that he had a son who grew up with no real place to call home.

He wondered if Eric or Mason left their wives alone to deal with their children, or if they were even married.

* * *

Days later, Carter found himself working on Delcia's roof. He hammered a nail into a shingle and wiped the sweat falling into his eyes with his forearm. He'd discarded his shirt an hour ago. If only he could shed the frustration of his desire for Delcia and his dilemma about David as easily.

"Well, that's it." Clay gathered up his tools and eased toward the ladder. "Come on in, Carter, and wash up for lunch. I smell soup."

Carter had seen only the outside of Delcia's house. Clay met him there as if he wanted to place himself between his daughter and Carter—or any man. The older man had every reason to worry. Carter wouldn't deny his attraction, but he wouldn't do anything about it either.

He and Clay had spent the morning on the roof repairing shingles displaced by the storm. Earlier, Pauline had taken Ranetta to the campground to get away from the racket they made. But the two had returned half an hour ago.

Since Delcia was at the campground, Clay probably deemed it safe for Carter to enter her house, she being well out of his range. He wondered if the older man planned to stand guard over her the entire three months Carter would spend in Coree? Of course, once he found his brother's murderer, Carter would be on his way.

Before David's death, Carter had planned to spend a few more years in the service, perhaps even ten. Now the security position he'd been offered wasn't as appealing as it had been when the offer was made. The idea of opening his own campground someplace sounded better by the day.

The out-of-doors appealed to him on an elemental level: the fresh air, less regimentation, but most of all mingling with campers. He'd gotten to know several families, especially those who were closest to his campsite.

He'd saved a portion of his money from every paycheck he ever made. When you came from a background of nothing, you tended to value your money. Carter had learned long ago not to be wasteful.

He gathered the trash and climbed down the roof after Clay. They entered the house through a utility room.

"You can wash up in there." Clay pointed to a closed door in back of the kitchen.

Carter entered a dainty half bath. Associating Delcia with anything dainty was a novel concept; he thought of her as capable, womanly, strong, but never dainty.

Tiny burgundy flowers splashed across the beige background of the wallpaper. He turned on the warm water and used the soap in the dispenser. A sweet scent tantalized his senses. He reached for the towel, then realized it was one of those pretty fingertip towels. His foster mother wouldn't let them use the pretty towels. They were for display only. She'd always put an old towel in the room for the family to use.

Damn, every thought brought him back to David. Another towel wasn't in evidence so he used the one provided and left, following the sound of cheerful voices to the kitchen.

Clay was sitting at the table playing with Ranetta.

Pauline planted her hands on her hips. "If you keep shaking her, she's going to throw up on you. She just ate."

"You're too sweet for that, aren't you precious?" Clay refuted, nuzzling her cheek.

"Let's see how sweet you think she is when she does. Go ahead and sit," she said to Carter and slapped a plate, napkin, and silverware in front of him. Then she stacked the table with a heaping platter of fried fish with steam rising from it, potato salad, greens, and corn bread. She reached for the child. "Give her to me and eat your lunch," she told Clay. Clay grumbled but handed the child over.

She set Ranetta on the clean floor and grabbed two glasses of ice tea from the countertop, setting one in front of Clay and the other in front of Carter.

"Thanks," Carter said. She smiled and retrieved a plate for herself from the cabinet. Keeping a watchful eye on her granddaughter, she filled her plate with food.

The kitchen was large and comfortable, with maple cabinets and a center royal blue marbled countertop. The same tile was used as a backdrop to the stove. It lent a country air to the room. The huge window over the sink and the French doors that led to the deck kept the interior light and airy.

Carter forked up the fish and closed his eyes in ecstasy. It tasted so fresh, the flounder must have been still slithering when she plopped it in the pan of hot grease.

"This is delicious," he commented and slid some corn bread into his mouth, stifling a groan. These islanders knew how to cook.

Pauline beamed. "Thought I'd give you a taste of our island cooking."

He increased the volume of his voice so it could be heard over the racket Ranetta was making. She'd pulled open a drawer and was banging old tin pots and pans together. All kinds of goodies looked to be stashed in that drawer. "You did yourself proud."

"Jesus," Clay complained. "How do you put up with that racket all day?"

"Just leave her alone. She'll scream the house down if we stop her. Otherwise she'll stop in a minute. I've been through this before." She glanced at Carter. "Does the noise bother you?"

"No," he said, though it was beginning to wear on his nerves.

"Well it's bothering me," Clay said. "Quiet, Rae."

Now that she had everyone's attention, the little girl started bouncing on the floor and looked at Clay with a toothless grin while she continued to bang two metal tops together.

"You just forgot what it was like having children around," Pauline reminded him.

Suddenly Ranetta stopped and Carter was grateful—and hopeful that the ringing in his ears would dissipate by night.

"I'm going to take the afternoon off and take Pauline to Morehead. We can start on the tables tomorrow," Clay said as Ranetta waddled to her grandfather's side. "What's that you got, sweetheart?"

She handed him a picture framed in plastic.

"Confounded. Why does Delcia keep that picture around?" He took the picture out the child's hands.

She screamed.

He gave it back to her and she made a way to her

grandmother on the other side of the table as if to put distance between herself and her grandfather. This was the closest she'd ventured to Carter. Ranetta was peeved at her grandfather for trying to take away her treasured picture.

"What do you have there?" Carter said.

Clay snorted. "Delcia should have thrown that bum's picture away ages ago."

"You know her feelings on that," Pauline warned.

"They're wrong. Rae doesn't need any memories of the no account . . ."

"Clay . . ." Pauline gave him the look millions of wives learned from the cradle.

Clay tightened his lips and hunched over his plate. The pose reminded Carter of Harry.

After careful thought, Ranetta meandered over to Carter, holding on to the edge of the table, beseeching him with gorgeous eyes. She shoved a picture at him containing many smudged fingerprints and a wet drool.

Smiling, Carter grasped one edge of the picture while she held on to the other edge. She wouldn't relinquish it completely. He glanced at the photograph that seemed to please her so and caught his breath.

A man wearing jeans and a sweatshirt looked as if he were taking a stroll along the ocean. His hands were planted negligently on his hips as he smiled into the camera, the ocean as the backdrop. He looked as happy and as satisfied as a man could look.

The image of David peered back at Carter— David wearing the mischievous smile, with his lips curled to the side, that Carter was so familiar with—David without his coin hanging from a chain around his neck.

Delcia stopped in the process of filing a reservation away and glanced out the huge multi-paned window to the left of the fireplace. Carter was hammering a nail into the table as if his very life depended on the force he extended. She'd watched him work for the last few days and he had impressed her as a precise and thorough worker. Something was bothering him and she wondered at the turbulence behind the power of those hammer blows.

He was an enigma. He watched her when he didn't think she saw him. Many times she wondered what he was thinking when he stared in her direction or at his surroundings. She wondered if he'd told the truth about his plans to open a park in Virginia.

She'd felt an abiding loss when Uncle Spike had died. It was probably the reason she'd taken up with Richard, because she certainly hadn't loved him, although she'd liked him well enough as a friend.

Delcia sighed, tearing her focus from Carter. Her dad and she still hadn't broached the subject that tore them apart last year. He was speaking to her again—barely. Perhaps he was as reluctant as she to test their tenuous truce.

"You're always watching him," Mark said, staring at her. She had to be careful around this cousin. He missed nothing.

"Just seeing what he's up to." Delcia finished filing the reservation and grabbed up another one.

"He's been doing the same thing for the last hour.

He's nailing into that board like the hounds of hell are after him." Mark answered the phone and Delcia continued with her filing.

"I guess he could be called attractive if you like an earthy kind of man," Mark said.

Mark definitely wasn't the earthy type. He loved his suits and ties. When she hired him, he made it clear that he wanted to work inside; he hated getting his hands dirty. This from a high school football player.

"Marcia home yet?"

"Yes, she is." Marcia had just graduated from UNC Wilmington, which wasn't very far away, just far enough for her to stay on campus. She came home almost every weekend. If she didn't, Mark would visit her there. Mark took accounting classes at the two year college in Morehead City. He hadn't planned to go at all until Delcia convinced him—he could still work full time and carry a light load.

"How are your classes?"

"Fine. I'm glad I let you talk me into going. Got only two classes left."

"Better to have it than not." She gazed at Carter again. He stopped hammering and glanced toward the building, his brows furrowed. He swiped a hand tiredly across his face.

What in the world troubled him now?

Six

Until the moment Carter came face to face with the photo, he'd convinced himself that the man who had fathered Delcia's child couldn't have possibly been David. Ranetta's eyes told another story, but in his heart he couldn't believe it.

David had stood by the very same gnarled tree whose roots sprouted above the ground. It was amazing how close the trees grew to the water. A few had even fallen during the last storm, their hold in the land fragile after years of combating swift tides.

Carter bit into his chicken salad sandwich, wondering why he continued to work here when he wasn't accomplishing any of his goals.

Now he ate at the employee's picnic table. Delcia had handed him a sandwich, fries, and a Pepsi after he repaired the last of the picnic tables and pointed him out here.

The door opened, drawing his attention. Delcia walked out. But she didn't have lunch and her expression was weary.

"Mom called," she said, sitting across the table from him.

Carter placed what was left of his sandwich on the plate. "And?"

"She said that Daddy was fussing about Richard's

picture. That you had seen it." She sighed with a mixture of exasperation and pride. "Ranetta is always getting into something."

"Does your mother know David was my brother?" Delcia shook her head.

He leaned his forearms on the table. "Why haven't you told your family about me?"

"They have their own worries. I'm not ready yet." Silence reigned for moments.

"I guess you believe me now?" she finally said.

Carter nodded. "It wasn't real until I saw that picture. I'd recognize that smile of his anywhere."

"As much as you want to, you can't make a freak accident into anything more."

"I don't believe it was an accident. Nothing adds up. Louise said that David was in Las Vegas at a convention when you said he was here. The weekends he spent with you, he was with her."

"None of this makes sense to me either. The paper said that David was engaged to be married. He'd promised me a month before that he was going to marry me. Of course, he was using the name Richard then." She smirked. "He changed names with the drop of a hat." She stretched her long legs in front of her. "You're wasting your money and your time."

"I'm paid up for three months. I'm not leaving until I find answers. Besides, Ranetta is my niece. I have a right to get to know her."

Delcia pounced, striking a finger in his chest. "I don't care about you and what you want. Ranetta is my baby. You stay away from her. I don't want her mixed up in this mess."

"I know you could never care about me. But Ranetta has a father and relatives on both sides of the family. David's not here to carry out his part of the responsibility. But I am."

Panic seized Delcia. "It's time for you to leave. You don't belong in Ranetta's life—or mine. We don't want you here," she said, hanging onto her temper by her fingertips. What would his intrusion in their lives mean?

"We'll talk again when you calm down." He stood at the table, packed up the discarded food, dropped it into the trash can, and ambled to the door. He stood there for a moment unable to even consider turning his back.

How crazy could he be? He should call Travis right now and accept that security position. He should put as much distance as he could between Delcia and himself. He didn't need a plaque with "brain surgeon" embossed on it to tell him why he was hanging around. Quietly, he opened the door and closed it after him.

Leave Delcia and Ranetta? Never, he thought, well aware that the two were mixed in his mind as a package. He wanted them both. Something about Delcia pulled at his senses. He wondered if the craziness would ever leave.

Something else bothered him—a sense of betrayal by David. Carter rubbed the back of his neck with his hand. That David could pull such a stunt tugged at the fabric of his heart. They were brother's damn it—a family. Honest, decent men didn't leave women with babies—especially children they knew about.

* * *

Delcia didn't know if she was scared for Ranetta or for herself. As much as she tried to convince herself that her heartbeat didn't race at the mere thought of Carter, she knew that it did. Carter was like a hot bonfire that attracted her and frightened her. She had no right to tell him to stay away. But suddenly, her world was closing in on her.

Marching to her office, she grabbed her purse from the drawer and froze when she heard voices from Ryan's office.

"Ryan, honey, you don't need to be here," LaToya simpered. "The park can be an investment. I know it's doing well. You're always booked. Business people make investments all the time. You can work in a corporate office in an area where there's culture."

"The island isn't a place for the cultural elite. It's a community of loving people who knew your parents, your grandparents. It's home."

"Honey, I understand that, but you can make friends anywhere. There are no art galleries, no theaters. What would we do for entertainment? This job consumes your life."

Who did she think they were? Delcia thought. *Country bumpkins with no cultural experience?* She enjoyed attending the theater just like anyone. Not that she'd had the time in the last year and a half. But when time allowed, she enjoyed taking in a good play and touring the art galleries.

LaToya was correct. The job consumed all their time.

"We have plenty of artists on the island. We even sell paintings and carvings here. As for entertainment, what's wrong with the mainland?" Ryan responded.

"It's not the same thing. My work is in Triangle Park. I love what I do."

"I love what I do here."

"But you haven't given the corporate world a chance. I'm just asking you to give it a try. That's all. If you find you don't like it, what have you lost? The park will still be here. You'll never know until you try."

Delcia heard footsteps and a chair squeal. She closed her hand around her purse. She imagined LaToya had left her seat to sit on Ryan's lap, thinking the promise of sex would change his mind.

"I'm not saying to give up the park. You will still own your share."

"I'll reap the benefits without putting in the work."

"Hire extra employees, silly, and pay them salaries. Delcia can manage."

"This is a small family business. It's different from a huge corporation. Delcia and I are the business."

"If it will make you feel better," she said. "You can come here one weekend a month to stay current in the business."

Delcia had heard enough. She shouldn't be eavesdropping anyway, but . . . well, there wasn't a good excuse for what she was doing. She imagined the idea of Ryan being a top corporate executive with an investment on the side would suit LaToya's self-image of being one of the upper class elite.

Delcia left the office, closing the door quietly behind her, and stopped by the desk. "Mark, I'll be back soon," she said. "I'm taking a lunch break."

* * *

Ryan caught up with her half an hour later. She had ventured away to her secret thinking spot. It was a private area of forget-me-nots, violets, and clover immersed in the trees. This was her property situated between her house and the park. But the park patrons never ventured as far as this small tree-covered area that jetted out toward the ocean. She sat on a fallen log that had been stripped of its branches and bark years ago.

"How did you know I was here?" she asked when a shadow blocked the sun.

Ryan sat beside her. "I've always known your hiding places." He stretched out his long legs, the sneakers peeking out from his jeans. He wore a Camp Coree T-shirt almost every day, as did most of the employees. Most times Delcia elected not to.

"And I've always known yours. Where's LaToya?"

"She left for home."

"I see." Delcia leaned back and looked at her ocean. She'd always thought of this ocean—as fierce and as unforgiving as it could be—as hers. Her private spot. Her sanctuary.

She knew that Ryan was working up the strength to tell her that he was leaving. She wished that he would have chosen a different setting—one that wasn't quite so personal, one that didn't have such fond memories.

Delcia couldn't shake the deep abiding sadness that had washed over her. She had everything she'd ever wanted, but there was some restlessness within her. She wondered if it was caused by her business, or her worries about Ranetta, or her father, or if perhaps she was suffering from delayed postpartum depression.

"I heard you in the office earlier," Ryan said.

"I didn't mean to spy."

"I know. Delcia, let's do something totally insane. Let's take the afternoon off. I'll get my boat. We'll go to The Point and drop anchor and fish or swim, or lay on the beach, or . . . whatever." He put an arm around her shoulder.

Delcia looked at him out the side of her eye. The idea was enticing, but they couldn't possibly. "We haven't done that in a very long time," she said wanting to convince herself to do the responsible thing—not frolic on the beach for an afternoon. Her parents had taken Ranetta to the mainland, otherwise she'd take the baby with them. But they couldn't leave the campground.

"I know. We need to get away. It's just twelve-thirty."

"What about the campground with loads of college kids?" Logic was called for, but the teenager in her wanted to shuck everything and take off.

"Barbara and Mark can handle it for one afternoon. Most of the students are hiking. We'll be back by evening." He lifted his arm from her shoulders, stretched, and leaned his elbow on his knee, giving her that mischievous sidelong glance. "I'll even ask Carter to come along. I feel guilty for all he's done and we haven't shown him our island hospitality."

Delcia's bubble burst. "I don't know about . . ."

"Ah, come on. I know we're training him, but he's gone beyond what he needs to do, what with helping with the roof repairs when I couldn't get away. And he won't accept money."

Before she could protest, Ryan snatched her by the hand and she found herself being pulled off the log and stumbling through the trees and marsh. "I'll stop by his RV and ask him."

"Ryan . . ." Delcia protested, taking running steps to keep up.

He didn't ease their pace until they reached the clearing. "Go on," Ryan said, laughing and steering her toward the store.

Digging in her heels, she glared at him as he sidestepped toward Carter's campsite, making comical gestures with his hands to get her moving. She laughed and shook her head. Marching to the store, down the road past campsites, she spoke to women lounging in the sun reading romance novels, men playing with their children, families dressed in bathing suits heading for the pool. Children and adults alike played rounds of miniature golf. A mother guided her son down the slide.

What a life, Delcia thought, as she picked up her steps. She felt more lighthearted than she had in weeks. Perhaps she wasn't suffering from postpartum depression after all. Perhaps she merely needed time away from work and worries—time to sit back and enjoy the world she'd created.

Back in his RV, Carter wrapped his hand around a warm coffee mug, staring at the steam rising toward him.

He'd made a royal mess of the situation with Delcia. Now he considered an approach to get her to talk to him more about David. The anger he felt toward his brother hadn't lessened. After David's behavior, it was a wonder that Delcia spoke about him at all. But he hadn't deserved to be shot.

He picked up his cell phone from the table and punched numbers that he knew well. The phone rang only once before it was answered. After sustaining a busted knee during a mission, his buddy, Wadell, had been forced to retire three years ago. Once you'd been a SEAL, anything else was second best and his friend decided to give it up rather than resort to being a paper pusher. "Wadell. How's it going?"

"Good, good. Back on shore for a while?" Wadell said on the other end of the phone.

"Actually, I'm retired." Wadell was of the mind-set that a man should stay with the SEALs until he was thrown out. It was the life.

"Get out of here. When?"

"Couple of months ago."

"Thought you'd be in for the long haul"

"Something came up." Carter gazed out the window. It occurred to him that he was starting to enjoy this view from the dinette. "Actually, I want to throw a little business your way."

"Anything."

Carter tapped his pen against the notebook on the table. "I want you to check out a name for me. Richard Connoly." I don't know where he lives but he could be a biologist and teacher at the University of Washington—that is if he exists."

"Hold on. If he exists?"

"Right. Supposedly, David used this identity last year."

"Your brother?" he asked incredulously.

"I'm searching for why. I don't know if Richard was just David's alias or if this man actually exists."

"Let me run it through the computer and get back to you. Shouldn't take long. Where can I reach you?"

"I'm at a campground on a small island in North Carolina. You can fax me anything you find," he said and gave him the number. He must remember to turn on the fax. He hadn't used it since he arrived. Carter gave him his cell phone number before they disconnected.

With his other hand, he fingered the chain around his neck. For the last twenty years it was a reminder that whatever happened in life, he was connected to someone.

"Carter?" The door rattled as someone banged on the surface. "You in there?"

Carter set the phone aside and answered the door to Ryan. "Come on in. Shut the screen and leave the door open." A swift breeze kept the RV cool.

Ryan climbed the stairs into the RV. "Delcia and I are taking the boat out for some fishing at The Point. We'd like for you to join us," he said, glancing around the interior. Carter had bought only the bare necessities. Keeping the place clean and picked up was easy. At the Roberts', he'd lived in fear that the next day living there would be his last and he'd be packing up to leave—again. A SEAL was ready to leave at a moment's notice.

"Sure." Carter's spirits rose instantly. Delcia would be there.

"Mind if I use your phone? I'm going to order a picnic from Wanda's."

Carter handed him the phone on the table. While Ryan made his call, Carter wondered what made Delcia change her mind about him so quickly. He decided not to debate the issue—he'd just be grateful.

Retrieving his windbreaker and hat from the closet, he locked the door. The temperature could be quite cooler on a boat with the wet ocean breeze hitting you in the face.

"We'll run by the store and then on to Wanda's to pick up the food."

"Why don't I pick up the food while you finish up there? Where do you want me to meet you?"

Ryan sent him a grateful smile. "At the dock in back of my house."

They left, Carter taking his bike, his spirits as light as the wind. One question nagged at him. After his parting with Delcia, why had they decided to include him? He worked with them but that didn't mean they had to include him in family outings. Once the work day was over, they usually went their separate ways.

Carter reached Wanda's at the height of lunchtime. All the tables were full, the voices lively. He retrieved the boxed lunch from the hostess and secured it to the back of his bike. From there, he rode to Ryan's house. He'd been there last week with Clay to make repairs. Carter veered to the back of the house and parked his bike.

The view was very much like the view from Delcia's place. He glimpsed the dock and saw the boat bobbing in the water. Delcia and Ryan hadn't arrived so Carter took the lunch and left it on the table while he sat on one of the lawn chairs under an oak tree in the middle of the yard. Instead of facing the ocean, he regarded the brick ranch house. Clay had said he and Pauline had built the house five years after they married—around 1970. They'd saved every cent Pauline made so they could afford to build. Clay's parents had lived in the house where Harry currently resided.

Clay and Harry's parents had purchased the land in 1905. The original Anderson homestead had been damaged in a storm in the fifties. By that time, they'd passed away and the house had been used for rental. A swing swayed back and forth under an oak tree. It looked as if it had been there for decades. Delcia and Ryan must have spent hours of fun on that swing. He saw a playhouse in the tree next to it. It looked old, as if it also had been built many years ago. He imagined Ryan and his friends there. He wondered if it was his friends' secret play area, or if he ever let Delcia enter his special sanctuary.

This was a wonderful place for rearing children, Carter thought. Delcia's house was close by, separated only by land and trees. The fact that Ranetta would grow up among relatives counting several generations back to the beginning of the twentieth century, sent a warm rush and at the same time left something missing in Carter's heart. She would have plenty of space to play without her mother having to worry about her playing in the street.

Carter heard the truck approaching the house. It stopped at the side near the garage. The doors slammed and in a minute Delcia and Ryan appeared.

The long dock at The Point extended into the inlet where the water deepened. Ryan moored his boat. Today they had the place to themselves.

They took out lounge chairs and coolers and set them on the dock.

"Plenty of rods for you to choose from," Ryan said to Carter. "Make yourself at home." He popped the cap on his beer and sprawled into his chair as if he planned to spend the afternoon there.

"Which is yours?" Carter asked Delcia as he looked through the rods.

"I'm not fishing just yet. I'm going to walk along the beach." She took a blanket and a small cooler with her. A few feet back from the water under a shady tree, she dropped her things.

"See you later." Shucking her shoes, she waved and walked slowly along the edge of the water.

Carter wanted to walk with her but thought it wasn't a wise move just yet. He chose a rod and watched the sway of her hips as she walked farther from them. He dropped into the chair and cast his rod into the gray water.

Carter lasted a half hour and caught two fish before he gave up and followed her.

It still bothered him that he was attracted to a woman who may have shared something very special with his brother, whether his brother appreciated it or not.

He stopped near her as she sat on an old log. The ocean water had washed over it countless times. It was a wonder the log hadn't been washed away by the fierce storms. Some things did survive the waters of the Atlantic.

"Tell me about David," Delcia said abruptly. "One day I knew I would have to search for his family if for no other reason than his medical history."

Carter didn't quite know where to begin. He sat

beside her. "What occurred with you was entirely out of character for David. That's why I find all this so difficult to believe—not that I don't believe you, but it's just not like him to have an affair when he was engaged. He'd been dating the same woman for years."

"He could have been sowing his wild oats just before he settled down. One last fling, so to speak. I was the unlucky recipient."

Carter shook his head. "It's more than that. The assumed name. Leaving you with a baby. Saying that he was a biologist instead of a pediatrician, which was his career. He was a fine doctor."

"If he was such a fine, upstanding citizen, then tell me why he lied?"

At a loss, Carter shook his head. "Both of us grew up in the foster care system without having a soul who really loved us. We agreed that if either of us had children, that if anything happened, I'd see to his children and vice versa. We didn't want to chance leaving children behind without security or love. David just couldn't . . ." He looked away from her out toward the peaceful waves of the sound. It was time Carter came to terms with the truth. David did leave Delcia and Ranetta.

For the first time, Delcia realized that he was hurting even more than she'd been hurt, and for some unknown reason, she wanted to comfort him. "He was one of the kindest men I'd ever met. We formed an instant friendship. He told me he was a biologist and he would soon leave for the Congo to record some unique plant life. Because of the fighting there, the small group he was affiliated with would have to keep a low profile. He felt that what he was doing was important—that some plant life in various areas on the planet could lead to cures for fatal diseases, and soon all traces would be lost forever."

"David thought like that, not about plants, but about children. Life was sacred to him."

"We dated for a few weeks before . . . well anyway, it wasn't until he left that I discovered that I was pregnant. I wrote to the address he gave me and in early February this year, he returned. He seemed absolutely thrilled with Ranetta. He said he wanted to marry me, but first there was something he had to do. He wouldn't tell me what it was. He was so secretive and he seemed worried about something. He wasn't the carefree man who left. When he asked me not to contact him again, saying that he'd be back for us, I complied. That was the last time I saw him until March when he was using the name David. He acted as if he'd never seen me before. It was crazy. Then days later, I read in the paper that he'd been killed in a shooting accident at his bachelor party. The paper mentioned that his fiancee was a fellow physician. Then I knew he'd played me for a fool. No wonder he didn't want me to contact him. What puzzles me is how he thought he could get away with it? He was right under my nose."

"None of this makes sense."

"Well, it happened," Delcia snapped with an angry thrust of her hand.

"I've called a private investigator friend of mine and he's investigating this Richard. If I didn't know that David was an only child, I'd think that he was a twin. But I have his birth certificate as evidence. If he were a twin, that information would be listed on the certificate."

"What did you mean earlier when you said you knew that I would never care for you."

Carter stirred on the log. "Nothing."

"Did you think that, just because you don't know your natural family, that it made you different somehow?"

Carter remembered the admiral's daughter. The admiral had made it clear that he hadn't worked so hard for his daughter to start at ground zero again. "Of course it makes me different," Carter said, unable to keep the bitterness he had long suppressed from creeping into his voice.

"If I cared for a man, it's him that I would consider, not his parents, not his grandparents. Because you are the man you are, you're not your father or your mother."

"That's easy to say."

"How many upstanding parents produce wastrels for children? After all, the father and the children can be a world apart. And that can be good or bad."

Carter was silent. He wanted to believe her. Most African-Americans started from scratch and believed they could go as far as they were willing to work to get there.

"You feel it, too, don't you?" she asked,

There was no sense pretending he didn't understand—he followed the conversation just fine. "Yeah, I feel it." The question was what he was going to do about it. The answer was easy. Nothing.

"My caution has nothing to do with you. I made a huge mistake last year. I'm not ready to jump right into another one."

"I understand."

Her eyebrows climbed toward her hairline. "Do you really?"

"Of course. You feel you couldn't trust my brother. Why would you trust me?"

"There is that. But this pregnancy has caused a rift between my father and me. Not that I let him run my life. I'm capable of making my own decisions. But family is important to me. Even without my father's warnings, I don't want to fall into the same trap I fell into last year."

"Well, then, we're both safe. If I pursued a relationship with you, I'd feel as if I was betraying my brother."

"Seems family means a great deal to you as well."

"I cherished what little family I had." He stood, trying to put some space between himself and her, and her perfume drifting to him with the help of the ocean breeze. "I imagine Ryan's wondering what happened to us."

Unfortunately, she stood as well. "I should put dinner together."

Dinner was the last thing on Carter's mind, but he really needed distance between them.

She dusted off the back of her jeans. Carter wished he could do the chore for her—for him, it would be no chore. He fixated on a leaf that had fallen in her hair. He reached up and plucked it out. She moved her head and his hand fluttered against her cheek. He knew he should move away, but the touch of her soft skin drew him closer.

He looked at her and the budding desire he felt was mirrored in her eyes. This was what he'd been trying to avoid from the very beginning.

Carter leaned over and touched his lips to hers.

Her touch was sweet, warm, and heady. He vowed to take this one taste and then no more. When he wrapped his hand around her waist to draw her closer, she didn't resist.

Carter pressed her body against his. He wanted to go slowly, to savor the sweetness of her. But instead he pulled her tighter into his embrace and touched his tongue to hers. He'd been waiting a lifetime for this. It felt so right, so extraordinary. He got a taste of what being truly home must feel like. This was where he was destined to be.

He ran his hand over her hips and pressed her even closer to his hardness. He was lost in her essence. Just for a moment a fleeting thought occurred. If only they were alone with no other considerations, they could explore this to their heart's content. He could have the lovely Delcia. She was all softness and curves. Curves that were probably more rounded since she had the baby.

The baby. Carter pulled back from her and looked upon her face. She was flushed and aroused. He lifted a hand and smoothed it along her face.

"If only," he said.

"Then what?" she whispered against his neck like a warm breeze caressing him.

"I like you, Delcia Adams."

She cleared her throat. "We should get back. You go ahead." She waved him on. "I'll be along."

"You okay?" he asked, stifling the urge to touch her again. Instead, he dug his hands into his pockets.

She nodded.

Carter turned and walked stiffly through sand that was sprinkled with bits of grass. He gulped in deep breaths, trying to get his emotions and his body under control. Seagulls squawked overhead.

This should be called paradise, Carter thought.

Delcia watched Carter take the cooler to the boat. It was five and almost time for them to leave.

"So, how was your day?" she said to Ryan. "Feel better now that we've languished the afternoon away?"

Ryan shifted his stance and inhaled deeply. "Much better."

"You do love to fish."

"It's relaxing."

Delcia silently folded the blanket. This was a wonderful island—a wonderful life. She loved the quiet. One didn't always have to be saying something. Sometimes the peace spoke for itself.

"I really don't want to leave this area," Ryan finally said. "I love it here. I love my work. I know people think I got into this business because I followed your footsteps, but that just isn't true. I loved camping trips with Mom and Dad. Even as a child, I could think of no better occupation. This is more fun than work for me."

"Oh, Ryan." Delcia reached out and touched his shoulder. "Tell LaToya that." But she knew that he already had.

He shook his head and dug his hands into his pockets. "She doesn't understand. She likes the prestige of suits, ties and corporate life. She doesn't like me wearing jeans everyday to work. She doesn't like the fact that I have to get my hands dirty with this job."

"Doesn't she understand that you're a business owner?"

"It's not a glamorous business like being a million dollar real estate agent, a bank president, a lawyer, doctor, or head accountant."

"You won't walk into that company as head accountant."

"No, but I'll wear a suit, and that's important to her. Delcia, can you see me in a suit and tie everyday? I could live that life if I have to, to survive, but I'd rather not."

"Have you told her that?"

"I've tried. But she doesn't understand. So it's either the job I love or the woman I care deeply about."

"Well, you better do more than care deeply about her if you're even considering giving up your livelihood for her. If you make this move, you do plan to marry her, right?"

"That's the plan."

Her brother didn't sound too sure to Delcia. "Ryan, take the time to think this through before you make your decision. Marriage is one of the most important decisions of your life. Be sure that it's right for you if you decide to take that step."

He picked up a towel and threw it over his arm. "I was thinking that Carter seems to like this. If I leave, I'm thinking that maybe we could offer to sell him a share of the park. That way you won't have to shoulder all the responsibility. I'll still work with it. But you need someone here full-time working with you."

"Don't worry about me. If you decide to go, I can handle it."

"I worry about you and Ranetta."

Delcia's spirits sank but she hid her feelings. "I'm a big girl. I can handle this. We can always hire more employees. That's not a problem. We can afford it, can't we?"

"It's not that. Do you know how difficult it will be to hire someone with the dedication of an owner? Small businesses are going by the wayside because it's so hard to find help that will stick with you because small businesses can't afford the benefits larger corporations can. It's a worker's market right now."

"We'll make it okay. You just concentrate on what you really want and don't let the park be a consideration."

Ryan stared toward the water. Delcia closed her eyes and rubbed her forehead. She didn't believe that Ryan loved LaToya. If he took that accounting position, he would be miserable. The decision was his to make—and his alone. She couldn't choose for him.

Seven

Holding two bags of groceries in the pouring rain, Carter struggled to get the key in the lock. The phone was ringing. He got the door open, dropped the bags on the table and reached for the phone. It was Wadell.

Eager for any piece of information, he slid his wet jacket off and hung it on the doorknob. His attraction for Delcia dominated his thoughts. He leaned against the closet door and waited with baited breath.

"Richard Connoly comes from a prominent family in Washington. He's a tenured professor at Washington State University. Someone in his department said that he's on some assignment in Africa. He's taking the summer off, but he won't be back at school before late August."

Carter ran his hand across his damp head. Strange, he thought, that the trip to Africa coincides with what Delcia had told him about the man. "Do you have a picture of him?"

"I'll fax it to you as soon as we hang up. Do you want me to continue the search?"

Pacing the small space in front of the stove, Carter thought for only a moment. "Yes, and see if you can find some connection between my brother, David, and this Richard. There's got to be some link."

Carter hung up and waited. . . . He glanced at his watch. Ryan was leaving tomorrow to spend two weeks with LaToya and Carter expected him to drop by in a few minutes to update him on some last minute details for managing the campground.

The fax buzzed and Carter waited for it to finish the transmission. He snatched the paper from the machine.

The picture was from a magazine article and only partially resembled David. He released the breath he'd been unaware he was holding. Dark wavy hair hung past Connoly's shoulders. His shaggy beard was long and unshaped. Apparently, he'd just returned from recording plant life in the Amazon. The article was three years old.

David wouldn't be caught with long hair, much less a beard. He'd always been clean-shaven. Carter had grown the occasional beard on vacation, glad to escape the chore of daily shaves, but not David.

Carter remembered his own first attempt at shaving. Paul had noticed a few strands on his chin one morning at breakfast and had tried to smother back a smile. "Looks like you're growing into a young man," he'd said.

Carter had squared his shoulders. The next morning was Saturday and Paul had taken him into the bathroom and handed Carter his own shaving gear. He'd shown him how to shave without nicking himself. Carter had cut himself three times that morning and wore the scars like badges of honor.

Carter forced his thoughts back to the problem at hand. How did David and Richard connect?

They could have gone to college together. Carter had met many of David's friends, but not all of them. He continued to scan the article. Connoly had attended university in Washington State, David in North Carolina. No connection there. Of course, the two could have met at some conference. David was always attending them. But they wouldn't necessarily attend the same conferences; their professions were different.

He thought of the Roberts. He really should call them. He imagined Nadine was preparing dinner by now. While they were in school, she'd gotten into the habit of fixing dinner early because he and David were always starved by the time they arrived home. Paul was probably fussing through the house, putting things in the wrong place.

When Paul had first retired, every letter Carter had gotten from Nadine lamented the problems of having a husband at home underfoot twenty-four hours a day and the new adjustments that had to be made. Not that they didn't love each other—they did—very much. The space each of them had maintained for so many years was no longer there. Carter imagined it was like starting all over again. He knew they'd work it out. They were too loving a couple not to.

Raindrops drummed on the roof. He gazed out into the wet afternoon and deliberated. He wanted— needed—to hear their voices.

Carter dialed the number he knew so well. Nadine answered on the second ring and was immensely pleased to hear from him.

"What are you doing spending money on phone calls when a good letter will do?" she scolded.

Carter smiled. She always fussed about him spending money on them. Every gift he'd purchased, she'd say, "You shouldn't have. Better to put that good money away for a rainy day."

Carter instantly realized how pleased he was to hear her voice.

He shifted the phone to the other ear. "Just wanted to see how you were."

"We're just fine. You taking care of yourself?" she asked, to which Carter answered that he was.

In the background he heard Paul ask who she was talking to. When she took her mouth away from the phone and told him, Carter heard him pick up another phone—the one in the bedroom.

He told them about the campground and that he'd like to bring them there for a couple of weeks on vacation during the summer. Nadine didn't sound too enthusiastic.

"I've got a fully equipped RV with built-in shower and bathroom," he told her.

Then she fussed about the cost.

"Got good fishing there?" Paul asked.

"Sure do. The best," Carter told him.

"I'd love that."

After they got the preliminary small talk out the way, Carter asked, "Did David mention a Richard Connoly to you?"

"I don't recall anybody by that name," Nadine said. "Do you Paul?"

"Me either. Course my memory isn't what it used to be. If he mentioned it to me he would have told Nadine, too."

"I'll call you in a couple weeks and tell you when I'll come for you."

"We'll be waiting. But if you don't want to spend the money for a call, you can always write."

"Phone calls are cheaper now. Doesn't cost as much as it used to," he said. "Besides, I like to hear your voices."

"Well, we love to here from you, too, dear. Still, it's more than a stamp," Nadine admonished.

Carter assured her that she had him there.

"Carter, you be careful down there, you hear? I want you safe."

Her concern sent a certain warmth through him. "This is nothing compared to what I've been through."

"All the same, I want you to take care. I worry about you."

"You shouldn't."

"It's a mother's prerogative."

Carter fell silent. A mother. He never thought of her as his mother. Always as his foster mother. Someone kind enough to take in lost children.

Carter always felt he needed to pay them back for what they'd done. He also realized they probably saved every cent that he ever sent them.

"The phone bill's adding up. No need in paying good money to those folks. I'll write."

They disconnected and he looked at Richard's picture one last time before he folded it and tucked it into his pocket. He snatched his hat off the table and went to the camp store.

Delcia stood behind the cash register taking lunch orders. The crowd was thin but steady. Carter waited for a break in business before he approached her.

She wore a pretty red blouse with her jeans today. She'd applied a subtle hint of bright lipstick and she looked particularly attractive. She wasn't fashionably thin, but a nice handful. Carter couldn't complain; he liked women with shape.

With a lull in traffic, she came from behind the counter and Carter handed her the paper, leading her to a quiet corner. "Wadell faxed me a picture of Richard this morning. Have you ever met this man?"

She took the picture from him and frowned. "No. You saw the picture I have. There's a resemblance, but with this hair I really can't tell." She continued looking at the picture. "There's something about the eyes that's familiar."

Carter had thought the same. The eyes. The photo was in black and white so there was no telling what color his eyes actually were.

Delcia handed the picture back to him. "Why would David pretend to be this man?"

"I can't answer that." He wanted to spend more time with her. She wore the scent he thought of as her own special essence. "Thanks for yesterday," he finally said to prolong his stay.

"No need to thank me. It was Ryan's idea, but I enjoyed it. That outing lifted a weight from my shoulders."

"Well, I've got to get back to work," Carter finally said.

She caught him by the wrist. "You don't have to do this."

He glanced intently into her eyes. "Yes, I do. As an uncle, I have a vested interest in what happened to Ranetta's father."

"I told you . . ."

He put a long finger against her lips, then took

it away, surprised as she was that he'd placed it there in the first place. "I'm only asking that I share in her life. I want her to know that her father's family loves her." He dropped his gaze to the bib cap he turned in his hand. "A child can never have too much love."

Delcia dropped her hand from his. He glanced at her one last time and left the room, the touch of her lips and hand lingering. He'd grappled for some time with this attraction to his brother's woman.

They had completed the repairs occasioned by the storm. Clay felt out of place now that he didn't have anything left to do. Pauline had put the baby down for a nap and come into the kitchen, joining him for a cup of coffee.

She set the coffeepot on the stove and sat at the table across from him. "Have you talked with Delcia yet?"

He shook his head no.

"Why not?" she demanded.

Anger surged through him, making him tense and defensive. "Because I'm still mad at her."

"Clay, we've gone through this before. You can't stay angry at her forever."

"I don't want to talk about this, Pauline." The truth was he didn't know how to approach Delcia after all this time. What would he say to her?—that he'd been a fool for shutting her out? He may admit it to himself but he'd be darned if he'd admit it to anyone else. They still barely spoke to each other, and he missed his little girl. Lord knew she wasn't a little girl anymore but he missed her all the same.

* * *

Delcia wandered along the water's edge with Ranetta, pulling her in the little red wagon she'd had
as a child. She'd repainted it in March when the
weather turned lovely.

The Atlantic was temperamental today, the waves
crashing against the shore. No placid water was this.
One day it could be as calm as a contented child
after a meal, the next as ferocious as a wounded
bear. Delcia loved this ocean in all its varying forms.
Ironically, she gathered some peace from its frantic
ebb and flow. Who would have thought that a storm
had brushed through mere weeks ago? As she well
knew, such was the spirit of the Atlantic.

Ranetta raised her hand. She wanted to be carried. Delcia picked her up and hugged her close.
She was so warm and cuddly and smelled of that
sweet baby smell that Delcia loved so much.

"You're such a sweetheart." Delcia twirled her
around to the sound of her child's laughter.

"You like that, hum?" Delcia said and twirled her
again and again until they were both dizzy.

Laughing, she plopped to the sand with Ranetta
on her lap. She picked up the pail and shovel she'd
brought for Ranetta to play in the sand. Ranetta was
still a bit too young to handle the toys well, but her
childish attempts at digging pleased her so.

Delcia welcomed this rare moment with her child.
The paucity of time spent together the last two
weeks displeased her immensely. She placed her
hand over her daughter's and guided the shovel into
the loosely packed sand, then they worked their
hands together in building a hill.

Ranetta carried her hand toward her mouth and Delcia stopped her just before she sampled the sand. That was when she saw Carter approaching them. He walked slowly toward them along the edge of the water with his hands in his pockets. He wore jeans and the camp's yellow T-shirt.

When he drew close, Ranetta clapped her hands and crawled toward him.

"Well, hi there." Carter plucked her from her mom and lifted Ranetta over his head. She bent and kicked out amid her giggles and screamed for more. Carter lifted her a couple more times and then sat on the sand near Delcia with Ranetta in his arms. Ranetta enjoyed every minute of it.

She was accustomed to male attention since Ryan had taken an active role in her life since her birth.

"Tell me about your family," Delcia said. Ranetta grabbed a handful of sand and once again Delcia caught it before she took it to her mouth.

"What about them?" Carter asked.

Getting him to talk about himself was like pulling water from a turnip, Delcia thought. "What was it like growing up in Baltimore? Are your parents still alive?"

"My last foster parents are still alive. We stay in contact."

"Where did you live before the Roberts cared for you?" Delcia asked.

Carter gazed directly at her. "I passed through a succession of families."

"I see." *What a terribly insecure life,* she thought. Delcia was still at a loss at what to say. He was clearly uncomfortable with talking about himself.

"You lived near the water. Did your foster father take you fishing?"

Carter nodded. "Yeah. During the summers we'd spend many Saturday mornings on the Chesapeake."

"Did you enjoy it?"

"It was the highlight of our week. David hated getting up so early, but once we were out on the water, he loved it. Paul was an early riser."

"What was David like?"

Carter thought for a moment. "He was one of the kindest people I've ever met. A little too kind, I thought. He was always bringing wounded animals home. I helped him build a birdhouse because he loved to feed the birds." He chuckled. "The neighbors didn't like it because the birds were always eating plants out their gardens."

Delcia bet he made the perfect older brother. "You always protected him, didn't you?"

The smile disappeared. "Yeah. He was smaller than the other kids and they liked to pick on him because he was different. He didn't like basketball or stickball like the rest of us. He liked reading and experimenting. He always knew he wanted to be a doctor."

Delcia could imagine him protecting his little brother. But for the life of her, she couldn't picture the warm man he mentioned as the man who deceived her. But then again, she'd been fooled by him. David had a way with children and people in general. At the campsite, the campers had come to like and respect him. Those who came regularly asked about him when he left.

"You were married before," Carter said, breaking into her musings. "Tell me about your husband."

A moist sheen gathered in her eyes and Carter thought she wasn't going to answer him. She and her husband must have really been in love for her emotions to flow so close to the surface after all these years.

"Bruce and I were perfect for each other. We started dating in high school and we married right after I finished college. He was a man of few words, but he always did little special things."

Carter's throat closed. "Like what?"

"Like on our fifth wedding anniversary, he took me to New York. I'd never been to Broadway. He took me that weekend. We stayed in Manhattan and saw three plays—one each night, and ate at the best restaurants. We visited the Empire State Building, walked to Rockefeller Center. It was really nice and so unlike him. He didn't like the city." Her face had taken on a warm glow.

Carter realized he'd never be able to compete with that love match. He wondered how a man could be so perfect.

That afternoon after Carter returned from the walk, he called the detective in charge of David's case, only to discover he didn't have any additional information.

As Carter grilled fish for dinner, he thought of how much his foster mother loved fresh fish.

Then a thought surfaced that had nothing to do with David. Perhaps he should marry Delcia. It would give Ranetta a stable home life. Carter hadn't found love so far, unless you counted Laurisa. He didn't know if he'd actually loved her or her beauty. Now Delcia—he could see himself settled with her for the rest of his life.

Not that he was the best of catches, but he would provide for his family. Not that she needed him for that reason. She provided for herself just fine. But Ryan was considering leaving and Delcia would need help with the park. Help that Carter was willing to give. He wasn't exactly poor. He'd saved well during his years in the military even without counting his pension. He wouldn't come to the marriage with nothing. Growing up poor, it was important for Carter to make his own way—to always be able to support himself. He'd held a job since he was eleven years old, starting with a newspaper route. Every morning, rain, snow, or heat he'd delivered his papers, first on foot and later he parted with enough money to purchase a bicycle. And he'd done it alone until he moved in with the Roberts.

Nadine would get up every morning and help him sort the papers before his delivery. And most mornings Paul would drive him through the neighborhood before he left for work. When he'd insisted that he could do it alone, they insisted that he accept their help. Carter smiled. They'd been good to him.

Carter thought of Delcia and Bruce. He realized he wasn't the perfect match for Delcia, but what were her chances of finding that perfect match twice in a lifetime? Most people never found it even once.

* * *

After a morning spent with Ranetta, Delcia took her complaining child into the house. Her father was sitting at the kitchen table.

"Well, aren't you a dirty one?" Pauline said to Ranetta and plucked her out of Delcia's arms. "You're all tuckered out. You need a nap."

"She had fun," Delcia said, smiling and waving to her daughter. Thank God the summer help was in place, leaving her time for her daughter and giving Ryan a chance to be with LaToya.

"I bet she did. I'm going to clean her up and change her clothing." She disappeared into the back of the house.

"Well, I need to change and get to work."

Her father glared at her and tightened his hand around his coffee cup.

What is it this time? she wondered but didn't dare ask him. She could do nothing right in his eyes.

"I saw you with Carter. He was holding the baby."

Those were the most words he'd spoken to her since their huge argument last year. She hoped he wasn't gearing up for another quarrel. She got a cup from the cabinet and went to the coffeemaker.

"We ran into each other on the beach," she said, pouring her coffee.

"Delcia, you've already got one baby to raise alone. You don't need to be thinking about another man right now." He stared at her with unrelenting narrow eyes.

"We were walking on the beach, not having an illicit affair. Besides, I thought you'd washed your hands of me. What is it?" she said, slamming the cup on the counter and barely missing getting burned. "He was good enough to help work around here but not good enough to talk to me?"

"Gal, don't you get smart with me."

She took the dishcloth and wiped up the spill, then flung it into the sink. She turned to face her father. "Dad, stay out of it."

He scooted back in his chair, hopped up and bent so that he was face to face with her. "Your life's already a mess. I've got the baby to think of. You did it your way once. I want him away from here."

They were almost eye-to-eye, nose-to-nose. "Well, that isn't going to happen until his three months are up. He's a paying customer. I can't very well tell him to leave for no reason."

"Oh, you've got reason, all right." He swiped the air with his hand.

"Your paranoia!" Delcia shouted. Then she lowered her voice. "He's David's foster brother. He's hurting from his death. He's looking for answers to what happened. Can't you understand that?"

Clay Anderson looked like he was about to explode. "He had the nerve to come here after what that boy did to you? Why should you give him any answers?" He punched the air with his finger. "That family has caused this family nothing but problems." As far as Clay was concerned, this estrangement from his daughter lay at David's door.

"You can't blame him for what David did."

"Looks to me like he plans to take up where his brother left off."

"He's hurting. He needs to be here. Can you imagine what it would be like for Ryan or me if anything happened to either of us? I know what it's like to lose someone you love and if being here helps him somehow—then so be it."

"If you won't tell him to go, then I will."

"You stay out of it. I'm not asking him to leave and neither are you." Delcia walked toward the door. "I have to change."

"Delcia . . ."

"This is finished. I'm not fighting with you any longer. Why can't you just trust me?"

"Because I don't want you to make the same dumb mistake twice."

"I consider Ranetta a gift. Since she's my daughter, it's my assessment that counts."

"There's a right way and a wrong way to do things," he emphasized.

"She's here, she's mine, and she's special."

"I agree that she's special, but how special is she going to feel when she goes to school and finds out other kids have daddies and she doesn't . . . hmm? This is a small community, Delcia. This isn't the big city where divorces occur as fast as the tick of a clock. I can't remember there ever being a divorce here."

"Oh, no! They run off and never come back, leaving the family to fend for themselves as best they can."

"Just like that boy you took up with. Tell me. How are your going to protect Ranetta when children start calling her names?"

Wearily Delcia ran a hand across the back of her neck. "You've got all the answers, don't you?" Delcia left with Clay sputtering after her.

Clay bit off a curse and stopped at the doorway. He and Delcia couldn't say two words to each other without fireworks going off. If he couldn't talk some sense into his stubborn daughter, then he'd handle things with Carter himself. To think he invited that traitor into his daughter's house to share a meal and all the time he was harboring secrets—secrets that ruined his daughter's life.

Clay stomped to the stove, refreshed his coffee, and wearily took a seat at the table. Fifteen minutes later he was still contemplating the dilemma when Delcia rushed through the room on her way to work. She didn't say a word to him.

Before this argument, they'd at least ventured into cautious speaking. Now there was silence again, and it was all Carter's fault. Why didn't he just rent a hotel room on the mainland, or park that fancy RV someplace else?

Pauline came in with a sparkling clean Ranetta. She got a bottle out the fridge and warmed it in a pan of water. While she rocked the baby in her arms, she gave him the eye that said she'd heard the argument between Delcia and him. A man couldn't even have a few words with his daughter without the women ganging up on him.

Clay squared his shoulders. Dag nab it, he was right and they all knew it.

"If I didn't have Ranetta in the bath water I would have come out here and knocked some sense into you." Then she took the baby to the nursery to put her down for a nap. Ten minutes later, she was back.

"You don't know when to stop, do you?" she said before she even made it into the room.

"I'm doing what's best for her." He stubbornly looked straight ahead.

"She's a grown woman, Clay. Let her lead her own life—make her own mistakes."

He balled his hands on the table. "She's making a darn mess out of it."

Pauline crossed her arms beneath her breasts. "We've had this conversation before. You can't run her life for her. You're making things worse between you two—and you're making it hard for her."

"A father can't always do what's handy. He's got to stand for something and stick by it."

"I'm not saying that you should give up your beliefs. We've taught Delcia the best we could. The rest is up to her, Clay."

"We're our children's parents until the day we die. Just because they're grown doesn't mean they don't need us," he refuted adamantly.

"They're adults, not children any longer. At this stage, you're interfering." Resigned to his uncompromising demeanor, she uncrossed her arms and neared the table.

"I'm counseling."

Pulling the chair from the table, Pauline shook her head tiredly and blew out a breath. "Just don't cause a breech you can't patch up down the road." She dropped into her seat and reached over to rub her husband's hand. "If I didn't love you so much, I'd stop speaking to you." She knew that he worried about Delcia. He was too stubborn to let his daughter make her own mistakes. He always knew what was best. The two were so much alike, but he couldn't see that.

"It's time for us to go home. Besides, Jenny and I are bumping into each other."

"When Ryan gets back."

"Now. That young man, Carter, is doing Ryan's work."

"Which is why I need to stay near. He's got no family. Where are his roots, his beliefs?"

"He'll make his own roots. He's made something of himself, Clay. He retired as an officer in the navy."

Clay sputtered. "And probably has a woman stashed at every port."

Pauline narrowed her eyes. "In your eyes, no man will ever be good enough for Delcia."

"Bruce . . ."

Pauline let out a ladylike snort. "You didn't like him either. You barely tolerated him for years."

"I'll talk to Ryan. See if I can get him back here."

"Don't you even consider bothering Ryan. He needs this time with LaToya."

Clay wiped a weary hand across his brow. "She isn't right for him. Why can't our children find good mates like we did?"

"It's their decision. We can't make it for them. They've got to make their own mistakes. Clay, Delcia needs some time alone. We're leaving tomorrow."

Pauline squeezed his arm and stood. Regardless of his interfering ways, she loved him. Always have, always will, but he and Delcia needed some distance between them. She prayed every night that Clay would find some way to come to terms with Delcia and Ranetta.

Eight

Carter and Delcia closed the shop for the night and he walked her to her car.

"Do you want me to give you a lift?" Delcia asked.

Carter shook his head and tucked his hands into his pockets. "The walk will be good."

Delcia nodded and fished for her keys in the bottom of her purse.

"Is something bothering you?" Carter asked.

Her head bobbed up. "Why do you ask?"

"You've been distracted all day. Ryan will be fine. I won't leave you in the lurch. Don't worry. I'll stay until he returns."

She nodded. "Thank you," she said quietly.

"Would you like to go to Wanda's for a little while?"

There wasn't much night life on the island. Wanda's place was the only thing open after ten besides the Seven-Eleven and a gas station.

Delcia thought about having to face her father at home and nodded. Ranetta was already asleep for the night. Her mother had called an hour ago saying the baby was sleeping soundly. "Why not. I'll drive."

Carter got the door for her and walked around to the passenger side.

It took only moments to reach the bar. The music

hit them even before they left the car. The place was half full, and they selected a table in a quiet corner. After asking Delcia what she wanted, Carter went to the bar for two beers. He didn't see the waitress.

When he returned with the drinks, he handed one to Delcia and took a seat across from her, leaned back in the booth and regarded her.

"What?" she asked, unconsciously swiping a wisp of hair behind her ear.

Carter took a long drink. "I'm waiting for you to tell me what's up."

Delcia looked down at the table and shrugged her shoulders. "Nothing much. My father and I are having arguments."

"Ryan said things were strained between the two of you. What's the fight about?"

She was silent and he reached across the table and placed his hand on hers.

"If I'm prying just tell me," he said softly.

"It's not that." She blew out a long breath. "My father grew up in a very strict environment and he expects us to toe the line. Let's just say he's disappointed about Ranetta."

"She's a beautiful little girl. How can he not be proud of her?"

"He doesn't like the fact that I wasn't married when I had her." Delcia picked up her beer and drank.

"Would marriage make things easier for you?"

Her eyes flew to his.

"Would you consider marrying me?"

"What?" she asked so loud heads swiveled in their direction. Her hand tensed under his. With the other hand she set the beer on the table. Some of it splashed onto the wooden surface. She dabbed at the droplets with a napkin.

Carter couldn't imagine where the thought originated, but now that he'd said the words, marriage to Delcia seemed a reasonable idea.

"I'll marry you."

"Without love?"

"Love is overrated," Carter scoffed. "I don't know what love is, anyway. I know I like you an awful lot. Can't you feel what's going on between us?"

She tugged her hand back but he wouldn't relinquish his hold. "Yes, but I'm not running away from one problem by taking on another one. It takes more than lust to sustain a lasting marriage."

His eyes hooded, Carter let go of her hand and picked up his beer. "You mean whatever you had with Bruce."

"In a sense. I'm not looking for another Bruce, but at least I want the man to love me."

"I see." Carter swallowed his beer and measured his words. "I know that I'm not the best of catches, but I won't come to you with nothing."

"I'm not mercenary."

He reached across the table and touched her hand. "I'll make you a good husband."

Delcia watched him with sad eyes. "I know you'll try. But will you love me?"

"I'll take good care of you and Ranetta."

"Love is what keeps you going when the times get tough. And times do get difficult. Marriage is hard enough with love. It's almost impossible without it."

"Millions of people marry each year in the name

of love. I just read an article that said more than sixty percent of marriages now end in divorce. Love isn't all it's cracked up to be."

"Once you've had it, you know the difference."

Her comment stabbed his heart as surely as if she'd plunged a knife into him. "Do you find me so unacceptable then?"

"No. I . . . care for you, more than I should." Her eyes darted to the window as if whatever was beyond held grave importance.

"But?"

She focused on him. "I won't marry a man who doesn't love me," she said with finality.

Carter swiveled the bottle around on the table. "Are you sure my background isn't turning you off?" He examined her face intently.

"I'm not a snob."

"I'm glad to hear that. Tell you what, then. Why don't we spend some time together? Would you be averse to my courting you?"

Delcia smiled. Carter didn't know if he liked the merriment in her eyes. "That's an old fashioned way of asking."

He shrugged his shoulders, examining the remains of his drink. "I'm an old-fashioned guy."

She nodded. "I'd love to go out with you."

Carter smiled. "Well, Ms. Adams. Put on your prettiest dress. I'm taking you to the mainland this Saturday."

"I don't think so. We have to work Saturday night."

Carter groaned. "Dating you isn't going to be easy, is it?" Suddenly the tense atmosphere was replaced by lighthearted banter.

"Nope," she said smiling. "Not until Ryan returns."

"What time do we have to be at the camp tomorrow?"

"Our summer help is here, so Barbara and Mark are opening tomorrow. We don't have to show until noon."

"May I take Ms. Ranetta and you for a walk on the beach tomorrow morning?"

"Why, Mr. Matthews. We'd love it."

Hot lava poured through Carter. He tried to believe he was dating Delcia for David, but he knew it was for himself. This woman had captured his heart in a way no other woman had been able to. He used David as an excuse because he still felt guilty for yearning for his brother's woman.

Carter contemplated the beautiful woman across from him. He already knew his feelings for her would never fade. He guarded his heart carefully. The question was, after her beloved Bruce, could she feel enough for him to let him capture a place in her life?

The next morning Carter spent an hour with Delcia and Ranetta in the backyard. Then Carter left, giving mother and daughter time together.

Delcia and Ranetta listened to the peaceful ocean current, watched the sea birds, and crowded in as much activity as they could until it was time for her parents to leave with Ranetta. Delcia had never been away from her daughter. Not even for one night. Right now, she felt like changing her mind.

She pushed Ranetta in her swing—the kind with music, specially made for babies.

Shaded by the oak tree that was midway between Delcia's house and the beach, they watched the herons swoop down along the water's edge.

Jenny's daughter had just had a baby and Jenny wanted to spend a week with them. They were due to leave the hospital tomorrow. Delcia had also promised her mother that she could keep Ranetta for two weeks this summer. Since her parents had spent the last three weeks with Ranetta and she was quite accustomed to them, Delcia reasoned that the separation wouldn't be too traumatic for her.

Delcia was feeling horrible and her child hadn't even left yet.

Sweat beaded on Delcia's forehead and she pulled the sweater off Ranetta, who must have been as hot as she. The weatherman predicted the temperature would reach the mid-eighties. Ranetta was as cute as she could be in her Camp Coree shirt and short overalls. Her plump legs were pumping in the swing.

"Well, there you are."

Delcia faced the house. Willow Mae trekked along the lawn to where Delcia and Ranetta stood.

Delcia lifted Ranetta into her arms and met her aunt halfway.

"Bought something for you." Willow Mae handed Ranetta a small beautiful white teddy bear Delcia was sure would be dirty in no time after Ranetta dragged it on the floor and through the grass and dirt.

"Willow Mae, you shouldn't have," Delcia said, as Ranetta took the bear out of her great-aunt's hand and clutched it in her own. It was the perfect size for her small arms.

"Couldn't let our girl leave without a present, now could I," she said.

"I guess not."

"Your mama said to bring Ranetta to the house. They're all packed and ready to go."

Delcia's heart sank as she walked around to the front.

Harry talked as her father stowed a pack of diapers into the car trunk and shut it. Clay Anderson didn't look in her direction.

Uncle Harry glanced at her and then at her father and tightened his lips. He started mumbling something to Clay that she couldn't hear. Her father threw him an angry glance and walked away.

Her mother bustled out of the house. "I've packed everything, I think. My goodness, I forgot how much you had to carry with a new baby. Ranetta and I are going to have the time of our lives."

Delcia held Ranetta so tightly she squealed.

Before Delcia had time to ponder and change her mind, Ranetta was packed in her car seat in the backseat of the car and her parents were driving down the lane. Aunt Willow Mae, Uncle Harry, and she waved until the car disappeared.

Delcia kept the tears at bay until her relatives left. Then she ran in the house, shut the door, laid across the bed and had a good long cry. She should never have promised her mom that she could keep Ranetta for two whole weeks.

After a run along the beach, Carter wiped the sand from his shoes on the steps and inserted the key into the lock.

"Hey, there," a voice rang out.

Carter looked past his home to see Randall and stifled an oath. The man was getting tiresome. "You're back," he said and twisted the key.

He pointed to the surroundings. "Got to take advantage of this good weather."

"Good fishing weather." Carter wished the man had a regular job like most men.

"Good catch, too. The winds were low today—didn't have to fight to keep the boat stable. Got enough for you, too. Join us. Eric's over in the camper. Mason's coming tonight after he finishes at the farm."

"Got plans for tonight. But thanks." Carter didn't have specific plans after work, but he wanted time to think and he valued his privacy. He didn't have the free time that Randall had. He was on a mission to marry Delcia. He needed time to plot his strategy and to consider his career now that he was settling down. The security position was relegated to the back of his mind. After working with Delcia and Ryan, he discovered he rather liked the campground business. He had reasonable savings to finance a business venture.

However, the problem with Delcia remained. If he moved away, how would he help with Ranetta? The child needed a male influence in her life. And the idea of Delcia courting a league of suitors after he left didn't appeal to him. Carter frowned, contemplating one man after another entering his niece's life. She'd probably call the men "Uncle so and so" until she was thoroughly confused.

"I see our football stars are back," Randall said, forcing Carter from his musings.

"What?" Carter faced where he was pointing.

"Bill Thurman and The Bull." He nodded to the campsite on the row behind Carter's where four boys, ranging in ages from about six to sixteen, looked out toward the water. "They visit a few times each year. Think I'll go on over and speak."

Randall headed to a gorgeous huge RV that was just a little smaller than a bus and called out. "Hey there."

The men and boys looked up. The expressions on their faces indicated that they were about as happy to see Randall as Carter had been. As Carter turned the doorknob, he only hoped Delcia didn't lose business because of Randall, the pest.

Carter entered his RV. By rote, he closed the door, made for a chair, and slumped into the cushions with thoughts of Delcia on his mind.

His heart palpitated like he was having a heart attack each time he neared her, like a teenager with his first girl. What was happening to him?

Carter reached for the chain under his shirt and absentmindedly stroked his index finger across it. What would have happened if David had married Delcia? Would he feel this attraction whenever he saw David and her together? Would he have avoided his brother because of his feelings for her? He'd heard about brothers falling in love with the same woman and thought it was a bunch of nonsense. How could this have happened to him?

But David was gone. And it was left to him to see to Delcia and Ranetta—especially Ranetta, the innocent party in this situation.

Suddenly anger swamped over Carter again. He was always protecting David. When kids picked on him in school because he was a thin, short teenager, Carter had always stepped in. Of course, when he reached sixteen, David suddenly sprouted up like a bean stalk and didn't stop growing until he'd reached six feet.

But when all the other boys were playing baseball, Carter was tramping through the damn streets with David, saving cats and dogs instead of having fun, knowing that somebody would pick on his scrawny brother. As always, Carter was there to protect him—just in case. And now he's had to give up a lucrative position because he had to find out what happened to him.

Carter picked his picture off the table and stared at the mischievous smile that was always David.

"Damn you. What the hell was going on with you? You have a baby out of wedlock, leaving her with no protection. Didn't our background mean anything to you?" he said into the silence, not expecting and not receiving an answer.

Carter wasn't going to find answers in the photo regardless of how long he gazed at it. He set the photo back on the table. Was the shooting an accident? Did a hunter, hunting out of season, shoot David? Was the bastard too cowardly to come forward?

Carter wondered if he'd ever find the answers he sought. Still, the answers must be out there some-where.

By degree he calmed down. David hadn't been affected by the foster care system as Carter had been, but still he knew how a child could get lost within it.

* * *

Carter dialed the number to David's old office and asked to speak to Louise.

"She and Dr. Spiedel are on their honeymoon. They'll be back on Monday," the receptionist said. "Dr. Wright is attending their patients until they return. Would you like me to make an appointment with him?"

"Did you say Dr. Louise Lester is married?"

"Yes, they married on Saturday."

David's body was barely cold in the ground, yet his loving fiancée had married.

"May I be of further assistance to you?" a kind voice said through the fog in Carter's head.

"May I speak to Sandy?"

"One moment, please."

A moment later the office assistant whom Carter had met a time or two came on the line. Carter identified himself.

"We miss Dr. David terribly," she said.

"Thanks. Your receptionist said that Dr. Lester just married."

"Over the weekend. I'm really sorry to bring you the news."

"Didn't take her long to recover," Carter said under his breath.

"Loss is felt more deeply by some than by others, if you know what I mean."

"I certainly do." Carter proceeded to ask her about David's health in the last year but she had no more information to offer than Louise had. "Thank you," Carter finally said, and placed the receiver on the hook. How could Louise have fallen in love with another man so quickly? And David's close friend? What the hell was going on? Then, too, he couldn't complain too much. Didn't David father a child with Delcia while he was engaged to Louise?

This was all crazy but Carter didn't have time to deliberate. He went to the cabinet and dug out the paperwork he'd received. He was executor of David's estate. He called Wadell and asked him to start a background check on Louise. Perhaps she had something to do with David's murder.

After he talked with Wadell, Carter showered and dressed in blue jeans and a gold colored T-shirt. He decided to walk to the camp store. He needed to work off the tension this new information had produced.

Delcia had dressed in a pretty gold blouse with her customary butt-hugging jeans that Carter just loved. But his desire for Delcia mingled with thoughts of Louise and her recent marriage.

A number of projects were waiting for Carter. *Good*, he thought as he engaged with the customers.

Hours later Carter rushed to the RV after work and headed to his shower. No one stirred in Randall's camp. Carter hoped he could get away without getting caught up with the man. As an employee at the camp, he felt he had to at least be courteous to them, even on his own time. Ordinarily, he'd tell the man to bug off.

Carter knocked on Delcia's door a half hour after she arrived home, and held out a sinfully rich red rose to her. Delcia closed her fingers around the stem and smelled the tight bud. She hadn't expected him but was glad he had come.

"You smell good," she said. "You made a hasty clean up."

"Us navy guys learn early on to clean up quick. May I come in?"

What was she thinking leaving him on the doorstep? Embarrassed, she stepped back. "Of course."

Carter moved from the door and followed her to the family room where she was playing *The Temptations* on the CD player. Several lit candles illuminated the room, their flames flickered and the honeysuckle aroma filled the air.

Carter glanced around the room appreciatively. The house had never been so quiet. Everyone was gone. Ryan, Ranetta and Delcia's parents. There was nothing to stop them from exploring their relationship—to their heart's content.

Carter had to fight down the desire that stirred within him. The moment she'd opened the door, he'd inhaled the scent of her sweet, perfumed body. Her loose hair flowed around her shoulders. She was soft and warm, fresh from the shower. She wore a sleeveless sheath that ran from her shoulders to her toes. He wondered what she wore underneath, or was she one of those women who didn't wear anything—or much—to bed? The thought made his blood run hot.

She looked vulnerable in the warm light of the flickering candles that cast shadows on her.

Delcia glanced at him uncertainly. "I'll be right back," she finally said, backing toward the hallway.

Carter caught her arm before she could escape. "You aren't going to change, are you?"

"Yes," she whispered.

"Don't," he said, perusing her from head to toe.

"It . . . it isn't proper to receive company this way."

He smiled. "You're a very proper sort of woman, aren't you."

"Not really."

He stroked her arm. "I'm not a proper kind of man." Was that his husky voice? "Delcia, I've been waiting . . ." he pulled her close, let his lips whisper along her cheekbone. He let his fingers run up her arms, hoping that she wasn't pining for Bruce. She'd said earlier she hadn't loved David. Carter only hoped she felt more for him. The knowledge that she still loved her late husband was close to the surface.

For tonight, however, Carter wouldn't think of David or Louise or the many dilemmas he faced. Tonight was his time with Delcia.

He straightened and looked upon her flushed face. "How long were you married?" he asked her softly.

"Eight and a half years."

"That's a long time these days."

"Not for island folks, it's not," she said, shifting her stance.

"I've noticed that life's different here."

She smiled a tremulous smile. "I hope you meant that in a favorable light."

"Definitely praiseworthy. I enjoy the slower pace. I like knowing the people I speak to in the grocery store and drug store." He slid the cloth away from her neck, kissed her bare shoulder with the lightest of touches and straightened to glance into her sparkling midnight eyes.

Her voice was soft and yielding. "That's why I never left. At any other location, I feel as if I'm lost."

He lifted his hand and brushed the hair from her face. "You'll never be lost, Delcia Adams. Never," he whispered and found her mouth with his lips.

He pressed her body close to his and felt the womanly lines of her softness against him. His body hardened even more than it already had. He ran his hand down her back to linger over her hips, pressing her closer to him, her breasts crushed against his chest.

Her soft hand circled his shoulders, her fingers playing their own special tune at the nape. Her touch sent thrills spiraling through him, enticing him to hold her tighter in his embrace.

He lifted his hand and cradled her breast, rubbing the nipple though the soft satiny fabric into a hard peek. He shifted positions and lavished affection over the other nipple until he heard a soft moan from her lips.

Splaying his hands along her hips, Carter released her lips, and basked in the kiss-swollen softness. He ducked his head and kissed the delicate skin of her chin, her neck, her shoulder. Bending lower, he placed soft kisses on her breasts and suckled the hard peeks through the smooth cloth. Her hands squeezed his shoulders, urging him on. Slowly, he released her hips and dragged his hands over her waist and upward, touching and lifting his hand to cup her breasts again.

Her sweet siren's song urged him to explore her more thoroughly. Dropping his hands to her thighs, he peeled the fabric up her legs like the skin of a forbidden fruit. Kneeling before her, he kissed the sleek length of her thighs, nipping and tasting her dewy skin, stroked and touched her naked belly, and kissed his way upward to stop at her breasts. Unhooking the front clasp of her bra, he spilled the softness within into his hands. He took a moment to acknowledge their soft, sensual beauty before he laved the dark areola and slowly captured a delicate nipple in his mouth.

Her cry rippled into him at that most delicious, intimate moment. He dipped his fingers to her panties and skinned them down when suddenly, and without warning, her fingers captured his hand.

He glanced into her eyes—eyes that were glassy and bright with wanting and desire.

"We . . . can't," she said as her tongue came out to wet her lips.

Carter didn't argue. He let her dress drop to her ankles and noticed the rose that stood out brightly against the snowy carpeting.

He closed his hand around the stem and stood before her. He traced the red bud along her ear and her throat to dangle at the V in her dress. Bending, he pressed one last fleeting kiss on her lips. He took her hand in his and pressed the stem of the rose within and closed her hand around it. Letting her go, he stepped back, scrutinized her for one lingering moment.

The walk across her family room floor was the longest in his life. He closed the kitchen door behind him and let himself out into the cool fog-shrouded night.

Nine

Desperately wanting a drink to cool off, Carter headed straight to Wanda's. Once there, he noticed the football players sitting at a table in a quiet corner, the same table Delcia and he had sat at last night. Carter made his way to the bar and took a stool in a quiet area, hoping that no one would bother him.

It was almost eleven, past time for him to be getting back to his RV. He and Delcia had made a date for tomorrow morning to tour the island. He ordered a beer and took a long drink. It helped little to cool his blood.

A black-haired sister, wearing a slim black dress and tall heels came inside, stopping long enough to scan the room and then headed straight toward him.

Carter didn't want company tonight.

"Well, hello there, Mr. Matthews. How are you?" She took a seat on the stool beside him, her dress riding up her thighs at least six inches. Delcia may have stolen his heart but he wasn't blind—not that he would consider doing anything improper.

"Not bad." Carter sipped his dark beer.

"Get me a Heineken, will you, Joe?" She pierced Carter with baby brown eyes. "Long night?"

Her identity finally came to him. She was Wanda,

the restaurant's owner. "Unmistakably." And getting longer by the second, he thought.

He couldn't get the feel of Delcia's soft, sweet skin, and her uplifted breasts, out of his mind. No doubt, he'd spend the night contemplating their brief passion. Her soft rounded curves fit as if they were made just for him. She was one sensuous woman.

She'd been right to tell him to go home. She already had one fatherless child, and she hadn't yet agreed to marry him. Passion was one thing they wouldn't have to worry about once they married. There was no doubt in Carter's mind that she would marry him. She wasn't a young kid who didn't know her own mind.

"Heard you've been spending beach time with our Delcia," Wanda said.

Carter nodded.

She quirked a perfectly arched eyebrow. "And working at the campground while Ryan's gone."

Carter figured the whole island knew that Ryan had gone to visit his fiancée. There were no secrets in Coree. He glanced around as more people entered the bar. "Got a pretty good crowd here tonight."

"It'll do. Weekend's better. Pete and I own it together. I work the restaurant days, and Pete takes care of the bar. He's out of town tonight."

"Sounds like a good deal to me."

"Works for us."

Carter stifled an oath when the door opened again. Randall and his party entered, Randall's loud voice carrying across the room.

"Hey, Thurman," he hollered.

Carter could imagine the men gritting their teeth.

"Let me go over there before he runs my customers away," Wanda said under her breath. She left the bar, intercepted Randall's group, and then steered them to an area several tables from the players. Carter wasn't so lucky.

"Carter, my man." He hit Carter on the shoulder. "Fancy meeting you here."

From the smell of him, he'd already had enough liquor for the evening.

"Come on, Randall. Let's take this table over by the window," Mason said.

He waved his friends on. "Go on. Me and Carter here are gonna chat."

"Don't let me keep you." Carter took another sip of his drink. If Randall wasn't one of Delcia's paying customers, he'd tell him to get lost.

He sat in the chair vacated by Wanda and asked the bartender for a bourbon.

"You driving?" Joe asked.

"Goody-two-shoes over there is chauffeuring tonight." He pointed to Mason. Mason probably had to return home for work tomorrow.

The bartender poured the drink. Wanda had disappeared, evidently not too worried about losing Carter as a customer.

Randall sipped his drink and smirked at Carter. "So I hear you're getting a piece of Ms. Goody Delcia."

Carter felt his body stiffen at the insult. "Delcia's a lady. Remember that when you speak her name."

Randall held up both hands. "Didn't mean nothing. No need to get uptight."

Wanda sidled up like the pro she was at the hint of trouble. "Randall, you've taken my seat."

"Did I now? Can't have that now, can we?" He swiveled in his chair and patted his lap. "Why don't you just park it right here."

Carter's arm reached out for Randall. Before Carter could intercept, Wanda grabbed him. "Why don't I escort you to your table?" She let Carter go and pulled Randall off the seat, not letting go until he was with his friend.

Carter watched the progress in case Randall gave her trouble. Once he joined his friends, he slid into the booth and Wanda left to speak to another guest.

Carter finished his drink and left. The bar wasn't such a good idea after all. It took his mind off Delcia, but she immediately dominated his thoughts once he left.

As soon as the sensual haze evaporated, Delcia's father's words reverberated in her brain. *Wanton,* he would label her. Oh, but when Carter's lips touched hers, she didn't feel wanton, she felt womanly and fulfilled. Well, not completely. The sensual storm had ended just before things went too far.

Delcia poured a glass of ice water from the refrigerator and drank half of it. Then she took the cool glass and placed it against her cheek, her forehead. Her body still vibrated with the impressions of Carter's touch.

In her room, Delcia pulled the covers back on her bed and slid beneath the clean cool sheets.

She was definitely coming to life again, she thought. Carter was nothing like Bruce. But then, she didn't know if she wanted another man like him.

She'd loved Bruce, and he her. He couldn't be replaced.

Carter had his own uniqueness and claimed a special place in her heart. And she liked him just fine—actually more than she should. Delcia turned toward the bedside stand and glanced at the rosebud she'd placed in a small vase. She flicked the lamplight out. Pulling the covers to her shoulders, she closed her eyes, with Carter on her mind and a smile in her heart. She compared herself to the precious rosebud Carter had gifted her with. She was opening up little by little and soon she hoped to be in full blossom.

The phone rang at seven. Carter had taken to sleeping until half past seven these days. He cleared his throat.

"Rise and shine, sleepy head," Wadell said. "Got news for you. Are you up?"

Carter swung his legs over the side of the makeshift bed, wiping the sleep from his eyes. "I'm up now."

"You sure?"

"Yeah," he said.

"Good. Louise Lester is flat broke. She's maxed out on her credit cards, and defaulted on a couple of loans. She went to closing on the sale of her house two days before she moved in with her new husband, Dr. Spiedel. Even the profit from the sale won't clear all her debts."

Carter was completely awake now. "What happened to all that money she makes?" he asked, moving to the table for his pad and pen. "I know they have equipment costs, but their office did very good business."

"When David was there. David brought in the patients. He isn't there any longer and they need a new star. They've lost patients since he died—lots of 'em."

"What about the other partner? Spiedel?"

"He's solvent. He's not a big spender, so financially he does rather well. But his patient count doesn't nearly compare to David's."

Carter tapped the pen against the pad. Anger stirred at the implication. "Did Louise's problems start after David died or before?"

"Well before. She's been in over her head for nearly a year."

"Not even David could have dealt with that kind of debt. Where's the money going?"

"I'm still looking into it. Just thought I'd give you an update."

"Got her new address?"

"Sure." Carter wrote as he rattled it off.

"Thanks man, keep me posted," Carter said and slowly disconnected, putting the phone on the table and thinking about the dear, nongrieving Louise. It was David's money she wanted all along. David must have discovered what she was really after.

Louise may be a cold woman, but she was also very beautiful and very crafty. A man not adept in the ways of scheming women was hers for the taking. Poor David stepped right into her trap and had no one to go to when he found himself in over his head.

No wonder Louise wanted Carter to hurry with David's estate; she needed the money for more than the office. Without the monthly bills, she and Spiedel would have larger checks to deposit in the bank each month.

Carter knew that Louise had come from a dirt poor family in a rural section of North Carolina and she'd graduated at the top of her class. With the help of a full scholarship, she made her way through college and received a partial scholarship for medical school.

Nothing wrong with that, Carter thought. Who from humble beginnings didn't have dreams for something better? He included himself in that group. It was admirable for students who knew they didn't have another way for college financing to do their level best in high school to qualify for scholarships.

What made Louise different was that she was a user. She knew she couldn't pull the clients she needed to aspire to greater heights with her skills alone. She'd seen depth in David and had latched onto him. Even Carter had recognized the something extra about David, and evidently, so had his patients.

Wherever he went, Louise was sure to follow. David's aberration with stepping out with Delcia put an end to Louise's dreams and her meal ticket.

He wouldn't put it past Louise to have David killed if she knew David was leaving her for another woman. With him dead, the insurance money was more than enough to clear up her financial problems.

A flash of pain battled with deep-seated anger. He hadn't been there to help David when his brother most needed it.

What man made of flesh and blood wouldn't want Delcia's softness rather than the cold Louise to look forward to each night? Given a choice, he knew his answer, and evidently David had finally seen the light.

Carter never liked Louise. Seems he had excellent reason not to, he thought, as he turned on the shower and let it stream over his head. He could picture her picking her way through the woods, shooting David in cold blood for the insurance money.

This new information still left unanswered questions. Why did David pretend not to know Delcia when he visited the campground? Carter shook his head. David's actions didn't make sense unless he pretended not to know Delcia because he thought he and she were in danger. If that were the case, why bring his buddies here for part of the bachelor's week?

In the shower, he finally remembered that David had even written to him stating that he didn't know Delcia. Carter could understand him holding the truth from others, but not from him.

Carter turned off the water, reached for a towel and moved to the small hallway to dry off. The bathroom was too cramped to move around comfortably.

Wrapping the towel around his waist, he went to the table and reached for the phone. He'd punched all but the last digit to Delcia's number before he stalled. He should postpone their date for this morning, but then he realized he couldn't do anything more until tonight. He may as well keep his date with her. It would be the only bright spot on this day, although his conscience nagged him once more about dating the woman his brother probably loved.

Carter pressed the off button, dropping the phone on the table. He dug out his map and searched for Louise's new address. Sitting at the table, he studied the map until the location was committed to memory.

Then he retrieved a black box he'd stored in a hidden compartment in the seat. He selected the tools he'd need for his mission and packed them into a fanny pack.

At least he was making progress, he thought, as he stored the map and started to dress. Lord knows he's tried to stay away from Delcia, but he had a weakness when it came to that woman. He hoped David would forgive him, because if David were here, Carter wouldn't consider perusing her. But David wasn't here and he hoped his brother wouldn't begrudge him this happiness.

David had had a loving and forgiving heart. Carter didn't have a worry as far as his brother was concerned. It was his own nagging conscience that tore at him.

Delcia and Carter steered the boat to the salt marsh. On shore, the tall, rich marsh grass swayed gently in the wind.

Carter debated whether to tell Delcia the latest development. His intentions were not to keep her out of the loop, but did she really need one more thing to worry about?

She picked up a snorkeling mask. With Ranetta gone, a certain gloom had crept over her and Carter wanted to bring her out of it. Of course she missed her daughter.

Another solution hit him. Perhaps if he involved her more in his research, she'd have something to think about other than Ranetta.

She skinned her shorts down her long legs. Carter had an unimpaired view of her bathing suit clad backside. The royal blue fabric against her dark skin was dazzling. He'd either have to look away, or it would be ages before he could undress. He turned to face the marsh and shucked his jeans and shirt, leaving them folded on the seat.

When he faced Delcia again, he saw she was watching him closely. With her backside still at the forefront of his mind, along with the new vision in the skimpy suit, Carter's body reacted immediately. Her rounded breasts enticed him. Before he could stop himself, he reached for her.

Though only hours had passed since he'd kissed her, it seemed like weeks, months. But her taste was a familiar thing, indelibly etched in his mind. This time, he dispensed no nibbling kisses. He thrust his tongue into her open mouth, tasting the sweet essence of her and felt her fingers tangling in his chest hairs, and rising to his shoulders. She worked him like a magician, driving his need to new heights.

He released her lips and darted kisses over her face, neck, ears, and smooth bare shoulders.

"Carter," she said.

"Hmm?" He returned to her lips. He took pleasure in tasting her.

"Snorkeling, remember?" she whispered, but didn't offer any resistance.

"Later," he said. Right now, snorkeling was the farthest thing from his mind.

She pressed her hands against him. Carter stepped away, and took several deep breaths.

She prepared herself for the dive.

Reluctantly, he donned his snorkeling gear. When Delcia was ready, they dropped into the cold water, dousing the burning desire that had embraced their senses.

Together they swam and frolicked. Time stood still as they observed small moon snails, whelks and Atlantic horseshoe crabs. The underwater world was a paradise in itself. Their weightlessness and the sliding of their bodies when they bumped into each other almost made them forget another life existed above the water's surface.

After they had their fill of the underwater world, they walked along the edge of the marsh, a rich source of food for many creatures: the fiddler crabs, salt-marsh snails and periwinkles. At the muddy bank they came upon two little boys, no more than ten, digging for mussels. Like eager children, they helped the boys with their digging and then moved on.

By the time they finished exploring, it was time to dress for work and return to reality.

It wasn't until closing that Carter broached the subject of David.

"I'm going to check out Louise's house tonight."

"You're going to break in?" she asked, appalled at the very thought.

Carter was instantly defensive. Such an action was

out of the question to one who grew up in a protected environment. Carter knew a different world. "Only to gather information. She isn't going to just hand it over."

"You're right there, but your motorcycle will definitely stand out. Plus it's too loud to go stealthily into a quiet neighborhood."

"You know the area?" he asked, lowering the lights for closing.

"My parents have friends who live there." They walked toward the front door together.

"If you don't mind my borrowing your car, it would be better. But I'd planned to park a few blocks away."

Delcia watched him carefully. "I thought I'd just tag along."

Carter stopped in his tracks. "You? Ms. Straight and Narrow?"

Delcia shifted positions and pursed her lips. "And why not? I can stand guard or help search. It'll take half the time with two people."

Carter shook his head. "Absolutely not."

Delcia planted her hands on her hips. "Don't shake your head at me, Carter. There's absolutely no reason why I can't go along. I know the area better than you do. I played there as a child."

Carter wasn't convinced. "I move better alone. You'll divide my concentration."

"Even SEALs work as a team," she said, glaring at him.

"Lady, you don't begin to know anything about a SEAL team. Nor do you have the training. If I needed to get away quickly, you'd hold me back."

"You said they were on their honeymoon. We'll have the whole night."

Carter wouldn't elaborate on the millions of details that could go wrong on a mission. They were on a quiet little street in a quiet urban neighborhood, not the wilds of Colombia or the Middle East. But the adrenaline that flowed through him was the same on any mission—that imminent sense of caution that took charge in the face of impending danger.

Still, if trouble came, he'd keep Delcia safe.

He glanced at her bright sunshine-yellow blouse and white jeans. "Change into something black."

She grabbed her purse and rushed to the door. "I'll only take a few minutes. Lock the door behind you."

Fascination with another world gleamed from her dazzling black eyes. Carter shook her head. She probably viewed this as walk on the wild side, he thought, as he followed her and carefully locked the door behind him.

"I need to pick up some things. Meet me at my place as soon as you're done."

Carter watched as she dashed to her car and tore out of the parking lot as if hounds were on her heels. So much for anonymity, he thought as he made his way to his place.

They arrived in the modest income neighborhood of old homes at ten-thirty. Carter would have preferred later when more neighbors had settled in for the night, but the last ferry to the island left at midnight and they intended to be on it.

First, Carter drove down the street. The porch light illuminated the front windows. No little security stickers stood out.

The house was situated in a small cul-de-sac. Lights were on in all of the houses. With the windows down, Carter heard loud music blaring out of one house. The others were as quiet as mice.

Carter turned around at the end of the street of well-tended lawns, drove to a side street, and parked in a slot near a stand of trees. He glanced at Delcia.

"You can wait for me in the car."

"You'll need surveillance help," she said as she reached for the door handle.

Carter was resigned to the fact that she wouldn't be left out of this. He caught her hand and placed the ignition key within. "If anything happens," he whispered, "you make your way back and drive away." Her hand trembled slightly as she stretched to tuck the key in her pocket and nodded.

"I mean it, Delcia. No waiting around for me. I can take care of myself."

"I hear you," she said, but Carter had a feeling she'd fight to the bitter end. He'd just better make sure nothing happened. He was uneasy about taking the straight-laced Delcia with him.

They walked through the wooded area that went up to Louise's house. Her place sat farther back than the houses on either side.

Evidently Spiedel had a green thumb. Grass grew thick and pretty flowers sectioned off outside areas: the patio, gazebo, a little spring with a constant flow of water. Flowing water kept mosquitoes at bay.

Ever cognizant of his surroundings, Carter heard

a dog bark in the distance. Crickets sang. Wind rus-
tled tree branches. Now and then, a car passed by.

In the low outside light, Carter glanced at Delcia
clothed in a black turtleneck and leggings. She'd
even dug out a pair of scuffed black sneakers. Energy and excitement mixed with a trace of fear vibrated from her. When she started tiptoeing, he
hustled her along until they reached the door. She
was as quiet as a mouse. Carter smothered a smile.

With her standing guard, he opened his fanny
pack and took out a lock pick. Observing the locks
on the door, he realized he hardly needed the so-
phisticated tools he carried. An amateur could get
into this lock with a credit card.

In mere seconds they entered the white house
through the kitchen unobserved, and closed the
French door quietly behind them.

"What are we looking for?" Delcia asked, glancing
around the room.

Carter closed the blinds and turned on a penlight,
aiming it around the worn cabinets and white stove
in the country kitchen. An old table with a large
bowl of plastic fruit occupied the middle of the
room.

If Louise had her way, they wouldn't be here long, Carter thought. "I'm not sure. Anything unusual." He
tugged her elbow. "Let's find her boxes. She
wouldn't have had time to unpack."

Using the outside light for illumination, they
walked through a formal dining room, a living room
and a small family room that had lots of furniture
crowded into it.

Must be Louise's furniture, Carter thought, and
climbed the stairs.

They came to the master bedroom first. A bed had been taken apart. A headboard, footboard, and mattresses leaned against one wall. A king-size bed occupied the center of the room. Two bedside tables crowded each side. There was barely room left for the mirrored dresser.

This had been a hasty wedding. Spiedel hadn't time to move his furniture out before Louise replaced it with hers.

"She threw the poor man's clothes out," Delcia whispered.

Hangers with suits were slung across a chair. Carter flashed his light in the small closet.

"Will you look at that. She's taken three-quarters of the closet." A side and a half held Louise's suits, dresses and slacks. "None of *her* clothes are thrown about the room."

"Yeah, well some women are greedy."

Delcia wandered over to the table. "At least she let him keep his table. Reading glasses, a Walter Mosley novel, receipts, tie clip."

Nothing was on Louise's side.

Leaving the bedroom, they walked down the hall to find a guest room and a third bedroom with a desk loaded with crates of papers. A single file cabinet and numerous crates were lined against the wall.

"These must be Louise's things." Carter closed the blinds and handed Delcia a penlight, pointing her to the file cabinet.

As she pulled open drawers, he proceeded to the oak desk and leafed through the first stack of papers.

"Nothing's in here," she said as she stooped by a crate along the wall.

Carter leafed through medical related papers that included articles from journals. He searched two more crates until he reached the fourth crate that contained bills and bank statements, stacked like little soldiers in order. One huge check was going to Derrick Lester monthly.

Delcia neared him. "Is this useful?" she asked. She handed him a letter. It read, *I know you won't talk to me on the phone. I just need one more check and that's it. I won't ever ask you for any more money.* It was signed, *Derrick.*

Carter glimpsed an envelope in Delcia's hand. He shifted the light to it. No return address, but the envelope was postmarked Tremble, North Carolina—the small town where Louise grew up.

Carter stuffed the letter in the envelope. "Put this back where you got it from," he said to Delcia, and straightened up the desk. Then he opened the blinds. They used the outside light to navigate their way to the back door. He opened the blinds in the kitchen and locked the French door after they exited. Then they left for the car.

Once they were on their way, Delcia faced Carter. Her heart ran in overdrive. "You don't think Louise killed David for the money, do you?"

"If she was desperate enough. Derrick might be a beloved brother."

"As kind as David was, he would have helped her if she needed it."

"True. David never cared that much about money. It was the work that turned him on."

"He certainly didn't dress like a successful doctor."

"And he cared for many patients who couldn't

afford his fee. That was always a stick in Louise's craw."

Delcia shook her head. Such a loss.

"Are you hungry?" Carter asked.

Delcia just realized that she was. Maybe the excess energy was responsible. She gave him directions to a barbecue place and they ordered their food from the drive-in window. They ate while they waited by the dock for the midnight ferry.

Ten

The next morning, Carter consulted the map for Tremble, North Carolina, a small town fifty miles west of Raleigh. Carter would take a day off to travel there.

He left the door open to catch the morning breeze through the screen. The day was predicted to be hot.

"Hi," Delcia called out before she entered the camper, swinging a navy camp bag on her arm. She wore a sleeveless white blouse, shorts, and sneakers.

He folded the map with hopes of hiding it before she saw it, mindful to take the time to appreciate her bare legs.

One look in her sparkling face told him she was still flushed from last night's excursion.

"What've you got there?" she asked, drifting over to take a peak.

"Nothing." Carter continued to fold.

"Were you looking up Tremble? I looked it up on my map last night. It's a pretty long way from Beaufort." Dumping her bag on the table, she reached for the map, taking it out of his hand and opening it.

Carter stifled a grown. "Now, Delcia. This could get dangerous."

"We did okay last night. You worried for nothing."

"We searched an empty house while the owners were out of town. Tremble is different. We could come face to face with danger. I don't know what I'm getting into yet."

"All the more reason for me to tag along. I'll have a cell phone to make an emergency call if necessary."

"By the time help arrives it could be too late," he reminded her.

"You know what I think?" she asked, planting a leisurely kiss on his forehead and patting his back. "You're a worrier. How'd you ever do missions if you worried about every little detail to this extent?"

If her motive was to distract him, it worked. Moments escaped before he found his tongue. "I had an entire unit backing me, not to mention the navy and the good old USA," Carter said tongue-in-cheek. He glanced from her toes to her head. "I don't think you pack that much security."

"I'm better than nothing."

"That's what I was afraid you'd say, however, both of us can't be away from the campground together. This will take more than a morning."

"We'll start out tonight after work and spend the night in a hotel."

Carter's body tightened immediately. Sharing a room with Delcia was this starving man's dream.

She beamed him a winsome smile. "I'll book two rooms for us in the closest hotel. We can contact this Derrick person first thing tomorrow morning."

Carter's fantasy evaporated like a cloud of smoke. "Oh, I forgot. You've got mail." She opened the bag and pulled out the contents, depositing them in front of him, and took the seat across the table.

With his bubble burst, Carter flipped through the stack of letters that had been re-routed from his navy address. They were the regular ads, a couple of letters from friends who didn't know he'd retired and . . . he pulled up short.

One was in David's handwriting. He flicked his sight to the upper right corner. It was postmarked a month ago. David died two months ago.

No one else had that scrawl that was uniquely David's. Everyone knew doctors couldn't write legibly and David was no exception. Carter glanced at the date and a blossom of hope welled in his chest to occupy equal space with the tightness.

"What's wrong?" came Delcia's voice through a fuzzy haze.

"This letter. It's from David."

"He must have written you before he died."

His eyes met hers.

"It's dated last month."

Could David actually be alive?

She hopped up and came to his side of the table. "Hurry up and open it."

Carter's hand shook as he tore open the letter. A small piece of paper with directions dropped on the table. Carter's attention traveled to the letter. Before he even read it, he glanced at the bottom to see David's scrawl. Then his eyes traveled to the top.

Carter,
   By now you think I'm dead. But I wasn't killed in that hunting accident. My twin brother, Richard, was the one who died. Can you believe I have a

twin? At least had. We're identical. I always knew there was something missing in me. Unfortunately, when I met him, it was already too late.

I've been hiding out ever since, because the person who killed him wants me dead as well. It looks like you'll have to save me once again, bro. Richard told me not to trust anyone, even the police, so I'm stumped. Remember that letter I wrote you about that strange encounter with a woman? Richard had planned to marry her. They have a child. I don't want to write too much in case this gets in the wrong hands.

Sorry to put you through the trouble and anguish. Tell Mom and Dad that I'm okay. They're worrying, I know.

If you get this letter, meet me in Greenville at a park on the river Thursday at noon. I'll tell you everything then. If I don't hear from you, I'll start this search on my own. I can't wait any longer.

David

If Carter was the sentimental sort, he would have wept with relief. Instead his hand clutched the letter and he reread it twice. Tremors still fluttered in his stomach. For a couple of months he'd believed his brother was dead. It was hard to actually change that belief in a few moments.

Carter handed the letter to Delcia.

"Unbelievable," Delcia said as she sank in her seat. "It's two of them."

Carter was speechless.

He retrieved the folder with his notes, snatched up the magazine image of Richard, and tried to see a likeness between the two men. Richard must be the father of Delcia's baby. He felt ashamed for the sudden rush of relief.

Carter smiled. He wasn't lusting after his brother's woman, after all. Then he frowned. David's brother was dead. His real brother, not a make-believe brother like Carter.

His work was far from finished. His tasks were to keep David alive and to find Richard's murderer before it was too late.

Twins, Carter thought. He recalled the sense of incompleteness David had always experienced. Carter thought the animals were a substitute for what had been missing in David's life, his need to nurture. But a twin brother had created that void.

Carter waited for the jealousy he was sure would come. But he didn't feel any animosity toward Richard. He wondered what kind of life Richard had led.

He would have to notify Richard's parents. Carter didn't look forward to the deed, but he'd wait until David was safe to make that move.

Then there was Delcia. Richard hadn't betrayed her. Although David asked him not to divulge the information to anyone, Carter trusted Delcia. She wouldn't tell anyone.

"Today is Wednesday," Delcia said quietly. "Tomorrow we'll meet with David." She reached across the table and patted his hand. "Are you okay?" she asked.

Carter smiled, hopped out his seat and grabbed her in his arms, snuggling her close to him. "I'm more than all right. My brother's alive."

Then he realized that her Richard had probably loved her. She had some coming to terms to deal with. He put her on her feet and leaned back with his arms still around her.

"Are *you* okay?"

"I've come to terms with Richard's death. But it's a relief to know that he didn't abandon Ranetta and me."

Carter let her go and they sat on the couch side by side.

"Now we know that Richard was murdered."

"Why would anyone want to murder him?" she asked.

"That's what we have to find out." He crossed his feet on the ottoman. "I'm glad your parents took Ranetta with them."

Carter could almost feel the wave of fear rippling through her. "Do you think she's in danger?"

"I feel better with her being away, is all. Right now, I can't tell if David or Richard was the target. This letter widens the playing field."

"Maybe we'll find out more tomorrow."

"Perhaps."

Carter closed his arms around her and held her close to his heart. She'd gone through so much since last year.

Only a few campers were left in the campground. Most of the college crowd were gone, leaving only a few hearty ones to enjoy the solitude. Friday the picture would be totally different. It was the first week of June, a time when families took long weekends to spend on the water.

Delcia and Mark were working with weekend reservations when Carter stopped by that evening. She gave him an apprehensive glance. Since reading the letter this morning, the day seemed to go on forever.

"How many sites are rented?" Carter asked, as they closed the office.

"We're a third full tonight. It won't pick up until the weekend." She left the desk and they walked outside.

One site had a line suspended from a tree, the clothing flapping in the wind. Some pieces had dropped onto the ground. A woman chased toddlers and clothing both.

Apprehensive, Delcia glanced around.

"Will you stop that?" Carter hissed. She abruptly looked at him, then started to stroll, her hand squeezing his.

"I called Mom earlier. Ranetta's fine. She even cooed to me on the phone," Delcia said, looking at him out the corner of her eye. "Carter I'm worried. Do you think she's safe?"

"We don't know that she's in danger. No one has tried to harm her so far. She's just a baby. I wish I hadn't mentioned it to you."

"I'm glad that you did. I'd want to know if something was wrong."

"So far, only David is the target."

They'd put their trip to Tremble off until after they met with David. Delcia knew she'd suffer through another sleepless night.

Right then, all Carter wanted to do was kiss her. He was still giddy, knowing David was alive. He couldn't hold back his feelings for Delcia any longer. They'd been crowding him for weeks. But it was too soon for her. She just discovered the father of her child was actually dead and hadn't deserted her, after all. She needed time to absorb all this new information.

Leaving her at the car was the most difficult thing Carter had done. He needed that walk home to cool off. "Call me tonight."

"All right," she answered before she left.

Carter was a patient man. He could wait. His world was right once again. He was terribly saddened by Richard's death. It would have been good for David to get to know his brother. But Carter couldn't control the joy of knowing that David was alive. He was determined to keep him that way.

Thursday morning, Delcia was at Carter's camper at seven.

"Seems like nothing is going to be normal again. It's almost time for us to leave for our meeting with David," she said.

Carter leaned toward her. *"We* aren't going to meet with him. I am. Everything's changed. We weren't absolutely sure it was a murder until after we read the letter. Now we are and I'm not putting you in danger."

Delcia ignored him. "We can fix a picnic. It will look as if we're going on a lover's tryst."

Carter shook his head. After a night of sleeplessness—thinking of courting Delcia—references to lovers were the last images he needed. The woman had him losing his freaking mind. "It won't work."

"It will work. I can be as natural as you can be."

He'd never said no to her. It was about time that he did. "No."

She scoffed. "We haven't had time to go on a

picnic, what with all the work and shortage of help. Now we have the time."

Lord save him from difficult women.

"I'll fix a nice basket. I'll make a big production about dragging around the shop missing Ranetta. That part I won't have to fake."

"You're not a moper."

"I can act like one."

"I'll pick you up in a half hour."

"Good. Most of the families will be out fishing or on nature hikes. We'll drive the park's jeep. It can get pretty muddy around the river."

Carter entered the store a little later. Delcia was playing the grieving mother to a hilt. "Why don't we get out of here for a while."

"And do what?"

She already knew the score. He decided to play with her a little. He neared the desk and leaned his forearm on top. "I thought we'd go for a picnic. We can pick up something from Wanda's." Carter contained a laugh.

Delcia frowned. "From the competition? I can fix up something right quickly."

He shrugged. "Since I suggested it, I thought I'd come up with the food."

"No need." She rounded the counter and headed for the kitchen while Mark watched them with a speculative glance.

"She really needs to get out of here," Mark said. "I'm glad you're taking her. She's been moping about all morning."

"We won't be too long."

He waved a hand. "Take your time. It's slow. I can handle this group."

"Thanks."

Delcia returned to the room with a wicker picnic basket filled to the brim. From the looks of it, she had enough to feed a small army.

"You think you packed enough?" Carter asked, taking the basket from her. It was heavier than he thought. What did she pack?

"It's just a little lunch," she said, leading the way to the door.

They got into the jeep and drove west towards the ferry.

After the ferry ride, Carter checked his rearview mirror constantly to assure himself he wasn't followed—he even took false turns. They drove to a wooded area where David had instructed them to go, and parked the truck in a public park.

Once there, they cut the engine, but stayed in the truck and rolled down the windows.

"Do you think we're at the right place?" Delcia asked when David didn't show himself immediately. "I don't see anyone around here."

"This is it."

She sighed and glanced around.

"Relax. He doesn't know what I'll be driving. He has to make sure it's me before he shows himself."

Five minutes later, a bearded old man walked into the clearing with the aid of a cane. He wore a well-worn straw hat. Nearing the truck he, looked into Carter's eyes.

Carter glanced first at David's face, then at his neck. He glimpsed just a small portion of the chain, the likeness of the one Carter wore, before it disappeared beneath his shirt. This was David. Carter gripped the chain around his own neck. He restrained himself from jumping out of the truck to greet him.

The tightness that gripped Carter receded by degree. There had been that lingering doubt that David was alive. But he'd know those eyes anywhere. Now, David's usual lightheartedness had been replaced with worry and strain. David had been through a lot within the last few months.

"Climb into the back seat," Carter said, glancing around. It took everything in him not to grab David and hold him in a bear hug, he was so glad to see him. Since yesterday, there had still been that nagging doubt that perhaps the letter was from an impostor.

David opened the door and hoisted himself up as if he were having problems climbing to the high seat. As soon as he closed the door, Carter backed out from his spot and drove toward the main road. "Delcia Adams, meet my brother David Washington."

Delcia turned in her seat and extended a hand. "Hello David."

David shook her hand. "It's nice to finally meet you. Richard loved you very much."

"Thank you for telling me."

They continued to talk as Carter navigated. Out of the way places weren't the safest spots for rendezvous, but David wouldn't know that. Carter had passed a few fast-food places on his way and drove to a crowded MacDonalds.

They ordered sodas from the drive-in window. At least the proprietors wouldn't come out ready to shoo them away for loitering. Then he parked the truck in an out of the way spot in the parking lot. He passed out the drinks and leaned against the door so that he could watch David as they spoke, while also keeping a lookout for cars entering the parking lot.

David had definitely lost weight. And he looked almost identical to the photo in the magazine of Richard, the difference being that his hair was shorter.

"Is the beard real?" Carter asked him.

David took off his hat and ran his hand through his thick curly hair. "Yeah. I decided to change my image."

"You look more like Richard."

His eyes clouded and he looked down. "Yeah. I wish . . . well," he lifted a hand and dropped it.

"What is it?" Carter said softly, wanting to protect him again just as he had as a teenager.

"I've gotten to know him through the notes Richard left in the small cabin he rented by the river. He'd left his life's history on the laptop he had at the cabin. He'd been living there for a couple of months before . . . it all happened."

"What did happen?"

"Richard discovered that we were twins and he started searching for me. He also knew that we were adopted. His adoptive parents told him when he was young, but they didn't know that he was a twin.

"A few years ago, he started to search for his birth parents and when he did, he discovered that our mother had died in childbirth. But the family she lived with didn't know her background. We were put up for adoption. It wasn't until a few months ago that he discovered we were twins. He also found our natural father."

"He's alive?" Delcia asked.

"His name is Howard Sommars. He lives in Morehead City."

"Did he contact him?" Carter wanted to know.

"He did, but he never heard from him. Richard died before . . . ."

"You actually talked to him once?" Carter asked. "Before the shooting?"

"He called the office and discovered that I was at a bachelor party here for the weekend. He called several hotels before he located me and told me that he would meet me at the camp—that he had info about our childhood and that we were both in danger. We were to cover each other's backs while at the paint ball range." David picked up his hat and twisted it in his hand. "But it didn't work out that way. He was dying when I found him. He was alive just long enough to give me the location and key to this cabin." He inhaled a long breath. "If he hadn't tried to warn me, he'd still be alive."

"You can't blame yourself for what happened. You didn't kill him," Carter said in a disgruntled voice.

"Still . . . to have found him like that and then lose him within minutes . . ."

"I'm sorry," Delcia said slowly.

He glanced wearily at Carter. "You've always been there for me, haven't you?"

Carter spread his hands. "What are big brother's for?"

David's eyes jerked upward, and he smiled that slight crooked smile for the first time. "Yeah."

Then he looked at Delcia. "You know by now that your baby is Richard's?"

She nodded.

"I'm sorry. I'll do anything I can to help out."

"Thank you."

Once again, he focused on Carter. "How is Louise? I would have called her, but I didn't want her in danger."

Carter and Delcia shared a brief glance.

"I hate to spring it on you like this, but we've got a lot to do to find Richard's murderer."

David leaned frontward, clutching the back of Carter's seat. "Is something wrong with Louise?"

"No. It's just . . ." He didn't know any other way to break the bad news other than coming right out with it. "David, she's married. She married Spiedel a week ago."

As if Carter had sucker punched him, David slumped back in his seat. "You're kidding?"

It hurt Carter to see the pain on David's face.

"Didn't take her long to get over me, did it?" David looked toward the roof of the car and passed a weary hand across his face. "So much for love."

"It won't make you feel any better for me to tell you that I never thought Louise was right for you, anyway. She never loved you, David."

"I know she wasn't the kind of woman you approved of. But she was kind to me."

"David, that woman is a barracuda. You were too blinded by your infatuation to see her for what she is. Hell, David you're so involved in your work, that you don't take the time to analyze the people around you. She used you. And that's the bottom line." Carter rubbed the bridge of his nose. "Thank God your estate is still intact."

"You haven't probated the will yet?"

"Nope. I wasn't going to make a move until I discovered who killed you. And you better believe she's been hot on my tail because of it. She needs the money. She's broke." Carter informed him of Louise's financial situation.

"Louise is at the top of my list of suspects."

David shook his head. "I know she jilted me, but she couldn't have killed Richard."

"You let me be the judge of that. You're too kind-hearted to make a rational decision concerning her."

"I'm going to talk to her."

Carter signed. "She's on her honeymoon. You're not going anyplace near her."

"I'm not sitting in that damn cabin waiting any longer. I'm getting involved. Richard was my brother."

"The best thing for you to do is hide out where they can't reach you."

"I'm not hiding out any longer."

Carter scowled. When did David become so difficult?

"Tell you what? Just stay until tomorrow. Delcia and I are going to check out a lead west of Raleigh. Someone by the name of Derrick Lester."

"Louise's brother? Why?"

"She was paying him huge sums of money monthly. Suddenly she stopped."

"How do you know all this?"

"We checked Spiedel's house." Carter told him

that Louise had sold her house and moved in with her partner.

Finally they drove back to the park to let David off.

"Do you have a phone?" Delcia asked him.

"No." David said, getting out the jeep.

"Take my cell phone," Delcia said. Digging in her purse, she extracted it and handed it to David. "In case you need to contact us."

They watched David disappear into the woods before they drove to the ferry. Carter felt powerless. He wished he could do so much more to help his brother through one of the most difficult phases of his life. At the same time, he realized David was a man who had to weather the storms of life on his own. Carter couldn't protect him forever, no matter how much he wanted to.

Eleven

That night after work, Delcia and Carter drove to a small inn outside of Tremble. The Down Home Hotel came into view around midnight just off Rt. 40. As Carter pulled into the yard, a pick-up truck cruised on by.

Colorful azaleas grew along the walkway to the door. To Carter's dismay, all the rooms had outside entrances. He would have preferred inside access since Delcia insisted on her own room.

Carter parked near the lobby and cut the engine. He gazed fondly at Delcia. She'd dozed off hours ago and was waking up slowly. The halogen light in the hotel yard cast shadows on her sleepy face. She appeared warm and fuzzy and beautiful. Carter leaned to touch his lips to hers. How he'd love to take her right up to his bed and love her through the night. Instead, he settled for stroking her abdomen.

"We're here already?" she said as she sat up. She stretched delicately like a tabby cat.

"Yeah. Pull yourself together while I get our rooms."

Carter stepped out into the warm night, which did little to cool his desire.

The air was still and muggy. Suddenly he missed the breeze ever constant on the island.

He selected connecting rooms for them and in minutes they had unloaded their luggage, and the small cooler Delcia insisted on bringing, into their rooms.

Carter took a shower in a bathroom equipped with old fixtures. After that he checked the white page listings for Lesters.

There were about twenty Lesters listed. Carter cursed. It was too late to start calling tonight, he thought, as he slid the phone book back into the bedside drawer and switched out the lamp. He fell into bed knowing sleep wouldn't be long coming tonight.

Three minutes later he heard a soft knock on the connecting door, seconds before he heard Delcia's gentle voice. "Carter, you awake?"

Rolling out of bed, he retrieved the jeans he'd thrown over the chair and stumbled into them. Delcia had knocked a third time, calling out in her soft, sweet voice, before he answered her summons.

She was dressed in an oversized T-shirt that fell to her knees. He imagined she wore shorts underneath, but he wasn't sure since he couldn't see them.

"Yeah?" he asked.

She glanced at him out of sheepish eyes. "I couldn't sleep."

Carter laughed. "I guess not. You slept all the way here." He started to invite her into his room, but decided not to. He wasn't in the mood for another night of heavy petting and then have her traipse to her own room only to shut the connecting door between them.

Still, the lamplight cast an intimate glow in the room.

"Perhaps we could talk about our strategy for tomorrow," she suggested.

"That'll only take a second." He leaned against the doorjamb and crossed his arms. "You'll stay in the car while I question him. And that's final."

Before she could protest, he held up a hand. "I'm not backing down this time."

"Well, you're in a grumpy mood."

Carter looked at her, all fresh-scented from the shower, midnight eyes wide and beseeching. What red-blooded man wouldn't be moody?

Her demeanor soon changed to uncertainty and she lowered her eyes.

"Woman," he said, "You drive me crazy."

Her eyes widened to his.

"No more crazier than you drive me."

Carter inhaled sharply and closed his eyes. "You shouldn't have said that."

"And why not?"

He opened his eyes to her fresh beauty. "Because you know how much I . . ."

"You what?" she asked, tilting her head to the side. Her mouth was all sexy and inviting.

Carter groaned. "Why won't you marry me? You don't think you can fall in love with me?"

"I love you."

Carter's knees weakened so much that he thought he was about to collapse to the floor. "Then why won't you marry me?"

"Because you want to marry me for Ranetta, not

because you love me," she said with serious intent. "Marriage to a man who doesn't love me is unthinkable. Sooner or later, you'll regret it or you'll fall in love with someone else and feel trapped. The emotional toll would put a terrible strain on the household. I think Ranetta will feel the sting more because it would eventually lead to a broken home."

"What if I loved you, Delcia? Then all those barriers would disappear."

Her expression was guarded. "Would you say you loved me to convince me to marry you?"

"Never," he said, approaching her and gathering her in his arms. "I think I fell in love with you the moment I saw you."

She hit him on the shoulder. "Now, I know you're lying." She struggled to get away.

The humor fell from his face. He held her to him, cupped her chin in his hand and shook his head. "I'd never lie about something this serious."

And then he kissed her. Long, thorough and intense.

"You know," he said in a husky voice, "I've been reading up about North Carolina. Seems we can just go to a preacher and get hitched."

Delcia glared at him. "I will not be married in some midnight parlor. Besides, I haven't said yes."

Carter nuzzled her neck. "But you're going to right?" He gazed at her and held his breath.

"Yes," she smiled. "I'll marry you."

Carter held her so tightly he squeezed the breath from her.

"I'm not for waiting months. Elopement sounds better to me."

"How about a couple of weeks. You think that's too long?"

"Hell, yes!" he shouted, but he relented. "Two weeks is all you're gonna get."

"Since when have you spoken with a Carolina drawl?"

"Since I'm going to be a native, I may as well fit in and learn the lay of the land," he said, sliding his hands down her hips. "I'm a quick study."

"I'll turn you into an islander in no time."

His voice deepened. "I can't wait," he said as he lowered his head to kiss her upturned face.

The next morning Carter dressed in a black suit. He left the jacket hanging in his closet. Pushing up his shirtsleeves, he grabbed the phone book and marked off the first ten Lesters for Delcia to call while he started on the second ten names.

The first two names Carter called were white families. They didn't know a Derrick. The third Lester was an older woman, and thinking he was a telemarketer, she hung up on him. Carter continued with the next name and the next until a child answered.

"I know Derrick, he said. "He's my cousin. He lives down the street in the brown house. It's the only brown house on the street."

Carter thanked him and hung up, scribbling the address on the pad the hotel provided. He lived on State Street, right off of Main Street, the boy had said.

Carter hopped off the bed and called out to Delcia. She'd left the connecting door open. "I've got a street."

She held up her hand as she spoke to someone on the phone.

He fashioned the tie around his neck and rolled down his sleeves.

Delcia appeared at the door. "I've got his exact address," she said, waving a piece of paper, then stopped abruptly. "You clean up nice," she said. "You wear a suit like you were made for it."

Carter grimaced. "Let's go." He ran a finger around his collar.

Donning his suit jacket, Carter grabbed her luggage off the bed and carried it with his duffel bag to the car and stored the pieces in the trunk. He'd already stashed the cooler on the floor behind the passenger seat. Once they were on their way, he turned up the air conditioner to full blast.

In ten minutes they were driving down Main Street. They first passed old houses, built during the early twentieth century. The structures were freshly painted and the lawns were well tended. About a mile further, the area began to change, but not drastically.

They turned right on State Street. After two blocks the houses began to deteriorate. The farther they drove, the worse the neighborhood looked. Listing porches hung on by a prayer. Peeling paint fell from buildings that were once white, yellow, green and blue. The jukebox blared from a country store. Young men hung out on the street corner. Freshly scrubbed children darted about the street, playing with their friends while they waited for the school bus. Backpacks lay on the chipped sidewalk.

"There it is. On the right," Delcia said, pointing to a house with a few brown paint flakes clinging tenaciously to the wall and a sign dangling sideways on a nail.

Carter glanced around at the men hovering in the store yard. He didn't feel comfortable leaving Delcia in the car. He should have left her at the hotel. Suddenly, a future filled with a lifetime of arguments flashed before him, but he couldn't summon one regret.

He parked the car in front of the house. "Keep the door locked," he said as he slid out the seat and shut the door.

Carter loped to the house, hopping over a broken step onto the porch. The front door was open. He heard the television blaring. He knocked against the screen door.

A man with a shaved head and a trimmed moustache appeared, scratching his scalp.

"Are you Derrick Lester?" Carter asked.

The man regarded him suspiciously. "Who wants to know?" he asked wearily.

"My name is Daniels, investigator for the Second Chance Insurance Company."

Weariness changed to puzzlement as he pushed open the screen door. "What does an insurance company want with me?"

"I'd like to talk to you about your sister," Carter said. Derrick didn't invite him in, and that was fine with him.

"Which sister?"

"Louise. She's under investigation for fraud."

"Louise?" he shouted. "No way."

"We believe she's been embezzling funds. I'd rather ask you informally rather than haul you into court."

"Louise would never do anything like that. You've got the wrong person."

"We've subpoenaed her bank account. Her records show that she has mailed you huge checks every month for the last year."

"She covered some bills for me, that's all. No law against that."

"What kind of bills?" Carter asked.

"Hey, man, I didn't mean to get her into trouble. But I know she wouldn't steal money. She didn't need to. She's rich. She can afford it."

His reply sickened Carter, but he kept his face expressionless. "What kind of bills?" Carter repeated.

Derrick shrugged his shoulders and looked away sheepishly. "I ran up a few gambling debts. I didn't mean to lose that much."

"Why would she sell her house to pay for gambling debts?"

"With all that dough she's racking in, she shouldn't've needed to sell her house. She told me she wasn't going to give me any more after the first few payments but Mama talked her into paying the rest," he said quietly, then turned defensive. "The people I owed were gonna hurt me real bad if I didn't pay up. But I've learned my lesson. I'm outta that now. I promised Lousie I wouldn't do it again," he said.

"One more question. Do you know anything about her fiancé's death?"

"David?"

Carter nodded.

"Louise was real upset about that. After he died she said she didn't know where she'd get the money to keep paying me because patients started falling off and his brother wouldn't release the insurance money."

"Did you kill him?"

Derrick stepped back. "Hell no! He was Louise's meal ticket."

"But what if she thought he was seeing someone else?"

Derrick smirked. "Louise made sure he never had time for other women."

Carter started to leave, but the young man needed to be informed of a few things, and it looked like Carter was the only one around to do it. It was too easy to judge from the outside looking in. "Contrary to what you believe, Louise doesn't owe you one thing."

"What do you know about it? She made it outta here, I didn't."

"Did some rich benefactor come along and throw a fortune at her?" Carter shook his head. "Just maybe Louise *worked* her way out of here. She knew she couldn't afford college so she got the grades so that she could qualify for scholarships. While you're sitting around gambling her home away, you think about the fact that it was *her* burning the midnight oil, studying instead of partying. It was *her* working through a damn hard internship after her medical course work. She earned what she got. I'm not saying that you have to take her route, just that you've got to stand for something."

"Am I still going to have to go to court?" he called after Carter.

Carter shook his head. "Probably not," he said, negotiating his path down the damaged steps. He didn't believe Derrick really heard one word he'd said. He also believed that as soon as this fright was over, Derrick would go right back to gambling again. What did he have to loose? Louise paid his debts. He didn't have to earn the money to pay them.

"Another thing," Carter said, turning back to the man who now watched him from the other side of the patched screen door. "Call Gambler's Anonymous."

As soon as Carter reached the car, he shucked his jacket and tie. He rolled up his sleeves and flicked open the top two buttons on his shirt and sighed. He felt almost human again.

"Well?" Delcia asked, as soon as he started the ignition. She almost sat on the edge of the seat she was so burning with curiosity.

Carter replayed the conversation as he wheeled the car around and started their journey to the island.

Her shoulders slumped. "We keep running into dead ends. What'll we do next?"

"Contact David's father. We haven't crossed Louise off our list. She may have felt pressured because of her mother."

"How awful."

"I can't believe I actually feel sorry for Louise." Carter knew if he found evidence that she killed Richard, his sympathy would evaporate in an instant. "She should have let Derrick find a way to pay his own debts."

"Gambling is such a waste. So much money lost so senselessly."

"Some people buy lottery tickets before they pay

the bills or buy food for their children. It's a real sickness."

"I hope he's going to get help," Delcia said.

"He'd better. According to that letter, Louise isn't going to pay any more money no matter how much her mother pressures her. She won't even talk to Derrick, and I can't blame her." Carter saw Louise in a new light. She was an enormously proud woman who worked hard through high school, college and medical school, and into a successful business only to lose her home because of a perfectly healthy brother who wouldn't take care of himself—and trying to please a mother who supported his actions.

Sometimes families can be a curse as well as a blessing, but where would one be without them? Carter thought.

Delcia and Carter stood at the ferry railing deep in thought as the boat made its way to Coree Island. Carter was thinking of the upcoming appointment with David's father. Carter wondered how the man would take the news that he had children from a tryst that occurred thirty-seven years before? His wife had died several years ago, according to Richard's notes, and David had a half sister.

Delcia shifted beside him. He slung an arm across her shoulder shifting her closer to him.

She smiled up at him. "What?" she asked.

"Here I was thinking that I'm a crazy man."

"And why is that?"

"Because," he said, planting a light kiss on her forehead. "I've got the most beautiful woman in the world in my arms. I'm the happiest man on earth.

And I'm thinking about an appointment with David's father." He kissed her again. "I must be crazy."

She grinned softly. "I'll take that as a compliment. But, Mr. Matthews, I'm not crazy. I was thinking of my handsome husband-to-be."

"See?" he said saucily. "What would I do without a sane woman in my life?"

"Spend the rest of your life in misery," she said with a merry twinkle.

"Without you, I would be."

Suddenly they heard shouts from the upper deck and Carter looked up. Several people were shouting and frantically pointing down. Carter shifted his gaze to the left just in time to see a car almost upon them. He shoved Delcia out of the way just before it hit him. He barely had time to jump before it crashed through the gate and both he and the car fell to the water. On impact, Carter's head hit the windshield. He was knocked unconscious.

Delcia was dazed from the impact of the fall. Everything came to her in a haze.

The pilot immediately cut the engine. Crew members took the end of the life preserver and dropped it into the water after him. It was several frantic minutes—she didn't know how long—before they hauled Carter's body aboard and started CPR.

Someone restrained Delcia, preventing her from going to him, and she was instantly transported back to her husband's death. A feeling of powerlessness crushed her. She couldn't take another loss right after she found her love.

* * *

When Carter came to, he was in a bed in a pristine room in the island clinic. Delcia sat in a chair beside his bed wringing her hands.

He glanced around the room. "Hey there."

She hopped up, flew to the door, and called in the nurse.

Dr. Grant, the woman he'd seen in the camp store when he first arrived, entered the room wearing a white lab jacket with a stethoscope draped around her neck. For the next ten minutes Carter answered questions as she shone light in his eyes, and conducted a basic physical examination.

When she finished, he asked, "Do you know a Dr. Howard Sommars in Morehead City?"

"Yes, I do. He's a neurologist. It will take a while to get an appointment though. He's always booked."

"I need to see him. Just for five minutes. It's urgent. Can you arrange it? It's about a private matter, not medicine and it's important."

She glanced at Delcia and at her nod acquiesced. "Does it have to be in his office?"

Carter shook his head, wincing at the stabbing pain that knifed though his temple. "No."

"I'll see what I can do."

"Thanks," he said as she left them alone once again.

"How do you feel?" Delcia asked him, stroking his arm.

He touched the white bandage on his head. "Like a car ran over me."

Delcia shuddered, the memory too fresh in her mind for jokes just yet. "It almost did."

"Don't think you're going to get out of marrying me that easily. I'm expecting to be a married man in fourteen days."

"You've got to . . ."

"Fourteen days, Delcia, or we go to the Justice of the Peace."

Delcia smiled. "You can't be hurt too badly if you're issuing orders, can you?"

"Shucks, this is nothing."

With that comment, Delcia wondered what kind of life he'd led as a SEAL.

"Mark said Mrs. Roberts called. He told her that you were in the clinic. I tried to return her call, but I keep missing her."

"Keep trying, please. I don't want her worrying about me. She's been through enough with David."

Delcia kept touching him. She couldn't seem to let him go.

"Aren't you supposed to be at work?"

Delcia smiled. It was plain to see that he wasn't accustomed to attention. "Everything's fine over there."

His eyelids closed. "I can't seem to keep my eyes open."

"It's the pain killer they gave you. Go ahead and rest," she whispered.

"Don't worry about me," he said as he drifted off.

Delcia knew he didn't think anyone should worry about him—that he wasn't worth it. One day, she vowed, he'd know his own value. He'd appreciate what a wonderful man he was.

* * *

The next morning, family descended on them in droves. Delcia's mother and father returned from Ashville. Evidently, Mark had called Harry in the wee hours of the morning, telling them that Delcia and Carter were barely hanging on by a thread. Harry had called Clay.

Packing barely enough things for Ranetta, Clay and Pauline had jumped in the car and made the long drive. Clay's eyes were wild, his face haggard, when he saw Delcia. He didn't say a word, merely turned and walked outside. Her mom ran to her and just about squeezed the breath out of her. Delcia was ecstatic to see her baby as was Ranetta to see her mom, although she cried because of the confusion.

Right after, Ryan drove up in his pickup truck in a mad dash.

Finally, Carter fell asleep and the foot traffic stopped. In the lull Delcia pulled her mother aside. "Carter asked me to marry him."

"How do you feel about him?" her mother wanted to know.

Delcia smiled. "I love him. It's a different feeling from Bruce. It's more intense somehow."

"You're older now. Have you set a date?"

"Soon."

Her mom stilled. "How soon?"

"Two weeks."

Pauline was horrified. "We can't plan a wedding in fourteen days."

Delcia shrugged her shoulders. "He wanted to elope."

"Oh, my Lord!"

They didn't get a chance to elaborate because the

nurse arrived to wake Carter and dispense medication. Right after she left, Paul and Nadine Roberts entered the clinic clinging to each other for support.

Carter was shocked. "What are you doing here?" he asked them.

"They told us you were hurt," Nadine said, peering closely at him and giving him a grand hug.

After Nadine hugged Carter, Paul eased her into a chair, she was shaking so badly. Paul's own hands were unsteady when they shook Carter's.

"You drove here?" Carter asked, knowing that Paul didn't like to drive at night.

Nadine nodded, tucking her purse by the chair. "All night long," she confirmed, sliding her chair closer to the bed. "Never seen so much traffic in all my days."

Her wrinkled hand took his. Carter felt the slight tremor. Both the Roberts appeared tired and drained. Carter was deeply touched that they made the trip for him. But he hated that they went through so much trouble.

"I want you to meet Delcia. We're getting married. You can stay a couple of weeks, can't you? I want you there."

"You getting married?" Nadine asked.

"How are you?" Delcia asked.

"Well, you're a sweet little thing," Nadine said, then looked back at Carter. "Of course we'll stay. We wouldn't miss your wedding."

"You're staying with me. Why don't you go to my RV and get some rest. Delcia will show you where it is, won't you?"

"Of course I'll show them."

"We will after we spend some time with you," Paul said.

Delcia excused herself from the room so that they could have some private time with Carter. "I'll be right outside when you're ready to go," she said.

Paul sat in the other chair. "You gave us quite a scare."

"Kind of shocked me, too," Carter said, still wondering how the car got loose. The workers always blocked the wheels of the cars in front of the ferry. This time, he'd been too consumed with Delcia and their newfound love to notice if anything was amiss before it was almost too late.

Too bad there wasn't a list of ferry occupants.

Twelve

By nightfall Carter was back in his RV with Nadine fussing over him. She served him his favorite meal of pork chops and brown gravy, fresh peas, and peaches for dessert. They sat around the large table situated in the middle of the RV where they could gaze out the huge windows. The table was made to be taken apart so that a regular size bed could be made in the space. The bedroom in the back also had a folding door that separated it from the other compartments. Carter gave that space to the Roberts.

With all the cooking, it had gotten so hot in the camper that Carter had closed the windows and turned on the air conditioner. He wouldn't leave it on for long—just long enough to cool the space down. The air bothered Nadine's arthritis.

"Delcia's father is a nervous fellow, isn't he?" Nadine asked.

"They haven't been getting on too well." Pauline had thanked Carter profusely for saving her daughter. Clay and thanked him, too, but with much reserve.

"I am very happy for you," Nadine said. "I think Delcia will make you a lovely wife."

"Thank you."

"This is a beautiful camper, Carter. Looks better than some homes."

"A regular house on wheels," Paul said, glancing around.

"Don't even have to go outside to shower. I just love it." Nadine had sashayed around and made herself right at home, and Carter was glad for it.

Carter thought he was made of tougher stuff, but the ache in his head screamed so loudly all he wanted right now was a soft bed. Immediately after the meal, he gathered his plate and started to get up, but Paul waylaid him.

"Nadine and I wanted to talk to you," he said.

Carter relaxed in his seat. "About what?"

"We want to adopt you," Nadine said.

"Adopt?" Struck speechless, Carter could only gape. He was thirty-seven, for goodness sakes. Couples didn't adopt grown men.

"Why?" he finally asked.

"To give you that security you never had." Nadine reached across the table to pat his hand.

Paul squeezed Nadine's other hand. "We loved you from the day you came to us. But you never believed that we would keep you."

"You kept waiting for us to send you away. There was nothing we could do to make you believe us."

"That was me, not you," Carter said.

"We didn't adopt you when you were with us because we needed the extra money to pay for clothes for you and David and so we could keep you, but thinking back on it, we should have gone on and done it anyway. Back then they took kids away from foster parents if they asked to adopt them. They didn't want them to get too close. We were afraid they might do that as well."

Carter was so touched he didn't know what to say.

"Well, anyway, Paul and I talked about it on our way down here. As soon as we get back, we're going to talk to some people and see what we have to do."

"You don't have to do that. You're the only parents I've ever had."

"Yeah, we do," Paul said, nodding his head.

Carter couldn't let them go through the trouble, but he'd deal with that tomorrow. "There's something I have to tell you, too, but promise you won't mention it to anyone. It's crucial that you keep quiet about it."

"Okay," they answered in unison.

"David is alive."

First shock appeared on their faces. Then Nadine said. "Are . . . are you sure?"

"Yes. I saw him day before yesterday."

Tears glistened in Nadine's eyes. Paul put an arm around her shoulder.

"Then, why . . . that was David. We saw him," she said, pulling a starched, ironed handkerchief out of her pocket.

"I just discovered that he has a twin brother. That was who was killed at the range."

"Oh, my Lord," Nadine said, the tears running freely now.

"Why didn't he tell us? Why'd he let us worry and grieve," Paul asked.

"Because his twin told him that he was in danger and to stay hidden until he could get some help that he could trust. David sent me a letter, but I didn't get it until Wednesday."

"Where is he?" Nadine asked.

"Hiding out at a cabin in Greenville."

"Who would want to kill him? He was always a nice boy."

"That's what I'm trying to find out."

"Do you think that's why you were run down?" Paul asked.

"I don't know. No one saw anything."

"Lord, have mercy." Nadine shook her head. "You be real careful, you hear?"

He smiled softly at her. "I will, but remember, not a word to anyone."

Grinning, the older couple bobbed their heads up and down like silly school children.

"And Nadine, throw those Styrofoam plates in the trash. No washing them."

Waving a hand, she shooed him along. "You just go on to bed and let me tend to the kitchen. I'm not throwing good money in the trash. They're in good shape. We can use them again."

Carter smiled. He knew he was home. Nadine had been parsimonious for as long as he'd known her. Tomorrow, he'd buy paper plates. With those, she won't have a choice. This was her vacation and he'd see that she treated it as such.

Two hours before, Clay Anderson disappeared into the campground with Ryan. The ladies had the house to themselves. Ranetta slept soundly in her crib—exactly where she belonged.

Delcia and her mom took turns answering the phone. The news had gotten out that Delcia was getting married. Neighbors, family and friends called to verify. Even the reporter from *The Coree News Weekly*, the island's paper, had dropped by for a confirmation and details. They planned to run an article in their next edition. They wanted a photograph, but Delcia promised to let the paper's photographer take wedding pictures and said he could use one of those.

In the lull, Pauline said, "We've got to start planning your wedding." She led the way to the den and grabbed a notebook and pencil. "Come on, Delcia, we can't dawdle."

"I thought we'd make it very simple."

"Have you called Rev. Hariston to reserve the church? Is it available?"

"He agreed to do the ceremony. I thought the campground would be an excellent place to hold the wedding and the reception. Right on the lawn where we hold the hot dog socials and bonfires. We can set a fountain in the area near where we usually put the bonfire. Besides, the campground is where I spend most of my time."

"How does Carter feel about that?"

"I haven't discussed the details with him yet. He's leaving it all up to me."

"Well, don't you think you should include him? After all, it's his wedding, too."

"We could elope for all he cares."

"Don't even consider . . ."

Delcia threw up her hands. "All right, I'll fill him in tomorrow."

Pauline wrote furiously across the pad. "Tomorrow we'll go to town to shop for a gown. You'll have to purchase off the rack. It's too late to have one made."

"That's fine."

"Is this his first marriage?"

"Yes."

"Then we should make it memorable."

"I think all weddings are special."

"Well, I will be forever grateful to that man for saving you. Your father too."

As far as Delcia was concerned, the incident was still too close for nostalgia.

"We better give Wanda a head's up on . . ."

The doorbell rang. "I wonder who that can be this time of night?" Delcia asked and went to answer it.

Wanda and Willow Mae stood at the door, Wanda carrying a huge book and writing tablet in her arms.

"Sorry to barge in like this, but your phone was busy when I called." She sailed past Delcia. "We need to work on this menu tonight so I can order the supplies and schedule extra help. You don't believe in giving much notice, do you?"

Willow Mae ambled in. "I came by to see if you want me to make the wedding cake."

"Bless you." Delcia said and hugged the shorter woman. The islanders raved about Willow Mae's cakes. The cakes alone would guarantee extra wedding gifts.

She adjusted her bifocals and put her purse on the countertop. "Is Pauline here?"

"She's in the den."

Wanda stacked her cargo on the table. "I'm going to say hi to her," she said and ventured in that direction.

"I'm going back to see her, too, although I can't stay long. I cooked up some food for Carter's folks.

"That was nice of you," Delcia said. "Where's Harry?"

"Harry went on over to the campground to pick a fight with your dad."

Besides Carter's injury, her father's attitude was the real rain on her otherwise happy parade. She wanted so much for him to march her down the aisle. "That's all they seem to do when they're together."

"I used to try to intervene, but they're kin. Blood's thicker than water, I say. And I'm not letting them get on my nerves anymore," she vowed. "Can't do a thing about your kinfolks anyway."

"Good for you." If only she could take those words to heart, Delcia thought. But saying and doing were two different issues.

Carter watched Paul and Nadine disappear through the trees. After breakfast, he'd talked them into taking a stroll along the water. He felt much better today and would probably take one himself later.

"Mom." Carter mouthed the unfamiliar word. "Mother?" he said and shook his head. *Mom's better,* he thought. "Mom, will you hand me the pepper, please?" he sounded out into the empty RV, and laughed at his antics.

Turning from the view, he went to look in the small mirror in the bathroom and snatched the bandage off his head. Gingerly he pressed around the raw lump with hopes that the swelling would shrink by his wedding day.

Wedding day, he thought, as queasiness and excitement competed for dominance. To think that he'd found the love of his life tucked away on this small island.

He closed the bathroom door and went to the cabinet by the stove for a paper cup and saw Randall climbing his steps.

"Hey. Heard you were laid up," he said opening the door. Without an invitation, he came in. Carter rarely locked his door when he was in the camper except at bedtime.

"Got banged up a bit," Carter said and pointed to a chair.

"I'm not staying. Just stopped to see if you needed anything."

"Nope, but thanks."

"Heard your parents are visiting."

Carter nodded. "Came in yesterday."

"Well," he said, opening the camper door. "Take care of yourself. Just holler if you need anything. I'll be here until tomorrow."

Carter thanked the man as he left, but was much more pleased to see Delcia park in front of the camper.

"Hello there, Ms. Delcia," Randall said, skirting around the car.

"How are you, Randall?"

"Fair to middling. Just checking up on our neighbor. You're looking good after your close call."

"I didn't get the worst of it."

"Good to know," he said and moved on to his own camper.

Delcia looked better than good, Carter thought. Today she wore a sleeveless lavender dress with low-heeled strapped sandals. The dress allowed him to appreciate her legs. She should wear dresses more often.

Carter held the door open as Delcia climbed his steps. Before the door slammed shut, he grabbed her into his arms. "It's a pleasure seeing my fiancée this morning," he said, nuzzling her neck and then searing her lips and tongue with his own.

Delcia almost melted into the burgundy carpeting. This was what she'd have to look forward to for the rest of her life. Not bad by half, she thought and gave herself over to his hot kisses.

"Well, a good morning to you, too," she said when he let her up for air.

"Indeed it is."

She glanced at his forehead. "You've taken off your bandage."

"Heals faster that way. How are our wedding plans going?" he asked, leading her to the couch.

"Mom's in such a tizzy, I had to get out of the house."

He wrapped an arm around her shoulder and held her close. "You came to the right place."

"Well, who else would I visit today but my hero?"

"Your pastor, maybe?"

"I talked to him yesterday when he visited the clinic. You were fast asleep."

"Since we can't elope, where are we getting married, may I ask?"

"How does the campground sound?"

He nodded with approval. "It's where we met."

"So, it's okay with you."

"Perfectly. In front of the fireplace?"

"I thought we'd make it outside on the porch. That way anyone who wants to witness it can."

They sat on the couch necking and talking until the Roberts returned.

"I'd love to bake some pies for the wedding," Nadine offered.

"Thank you. My mother and aunt are busily working on the plans at my house. Would you like to meet them? They'd love to have your input."

"Oh, I'd be pleased."

"I'll take you there."

"Let me freshen up and grab my purse. I'll be right with you."

Paul shook his head as he watched his wife leave the room. "Son, you don't want to get near them til after the wedding. Things are gonna get crazy."

Carter glanced at Delcia with a teasing glint in his eye. "Just don't you get too tired to enjoy our wedding."

She laughed. "I won't."

Dr. Howard Sommars' height, light complexion, curly hair and green eyes were the same as David's, but his facial features were very different, Carter thought when he and Delcia met him the next morning. They were in the cafe on the first floor of his office building. He wore a dark blue suit with a white shirt and paisley tie. He looked uncomfortable in the getup, as uncomfortable as David usually appeared. David rarely wore a jacket. On a summer day, he'd wear a polo shirt and slacks. He always said the children were more comfortable with him in the more casual attire.

"Dr. Sommars?" Carter asked. The man turned to him. "I'm Carter Matthews. This is my fiancée,

Delcia Adams." Carter extended his hand and the doctor gave a quick shake and glanced at his watch.

"I'm only seeing you because of my respect for Dr. Grant. You've got exactly five minutes," he said.

"Thank you for seeing us. We won't take long."

He motioned them to a cafe table out of the traffic of people swarming in for coffee, bagels, or juice.

"How may I help you?" he asked after they settled in the small chairs.

"I'm representing Richard Connoly. I understand that he contacted you a few months ago."

"That name doesn't seem familiar."

"He thought that you may be his father," Carter said.

Recognition dawned and he nodded. "Oh, yes. I remember now. I was quite ill at that time and I got my son-in-law to look into the matter. He said the young man was an impostor, that he was only trying to swindle money out of me. He took care of the matter."

"Richard Connoly was from a prominent family. He was a professor at Washington State University with a doctorate in Biology."

His eyebrows rose toward his hairline. "Was?"

"He was murdered in March."

"Murdered!"

"Yes. And I'm trying to discover why. In his effects was research on his natural father. Evidently there was something in his mother's notes that led to you. He was unable to discover his mother's identity. She used an assumed name," Carter told him. "He was put up for adoption soon after birth. His mother died in childbirth."

"How old was he?"

"Thirty-seven."

His eyes clouded as he counted back the years.

"So it's possible that he's your son?" Delcia asked.

"It's not impossible. I was an intern at John Hopkins. It was just one occasion."

"Famous last words," Carter said. Glancing at the clock on the wall, he realized five minutes had passed.

The doctor's head darted up. "What is that supposed to mean?"

"It means," Delcia said. "That the same thing occurred with Richard and me."

"You have a child by this young man?"

She nodded.

"I'd like to see this evidence," he said. "If the evidence shows that I may be his father, then I'm willing to take the blood tests to confirm it and I'll divulge her name. I've never met her family, but I know where they live." Abject sadness crept over his features. "If that young man was my son, I want to know. I'll help you in any way I can to find his murderer."

"You also may want to find out what information your son-in-law used to base his conclusions on, because they were wrong. Richard was no swindler."

Carter thought for a moment. "Would you be willing to meet us after your appointments today?"

"I have an early day because of a seminar I had planned to attend this afternoon. I can cancel that. How does noon sound?"

"Perfect. Richard has a twin named David. I'll take you to meet him." Carter said. "And doctor, don't tell anyone about our meeting—including your son-in-law. I don't want my fiancée put in danger."

Dr. Sommars rose from his seat. "I won't." Carter and Delcia walked with him out of the shop. He headed to the bank of elevators to the left. Carter and Delcia left the building.

"I'll cancel my shopping trip with Mom. We were going to look at wedding dresses today."

"You can still shop. I'll meet with him this afternoon."

"Carter, you still aren't well."

"Lady, I have fought battles in much worse shape than this." He kissed the tip of her nose. "Pick out the prettiest gown you can find." He grasped her hand and kissed her knuckles. "Thanks for getting Mom involved in the wedding. She's thrilled," he said. Then Carter stopped. This was the first time he'd referred to Nadine as "Mom" outside of his practice attempts. He realized that Mom sounded right. Actually it felt darn good.

"It's your wedding, too, silly."

Thirteen

Carter kissed Delcia good-bye at the medical building at noon. Dr. Sommars met him at the entrance.

"Hope you've got wheels," Carter said. "My ride just left."

"This way." Sommars pointed to the bank of cars closest to the building. His had a reserved sign in the space beside a gray Mercedes.

"Where are we headed," the doctor asked once they'd settled into the soft leather cushions.

"Northwest on 70."

"How far?"

"Greenville."

The older man's hand clenched on the wheel. "Tell me about David."

Carter started from the time he met David to the present. By the time he finished the tale, they had pulled up in front of a primitive log cabin in the forest.

When father and son met, Carter could immediately see the resemblance by the posture, build, green eyes, and facial expressions. Even time and distance failed to erase inherent genetic factors.

While the men got acquainted, Carter called Detective Stubbs to let him know that David was alive and that Richard Connoly was the murder victim. The detective met them at the cabin an hour later. This put an entirely new light on the murder.

The detective interviewed both David and Carter and took some of the papers Richard had left, promising to return them at a later time.

As Carter knew and dreaded all along, Richard's adoptive parents in Washington had to be notified immediately.

Dealing with in-laws was tricky business, Carter thought the next morning. You couldn't just give them a piece of your mind if you thought they were acting like idiots. A prospective groom was required to handle the situation in a way that would preserve the family relationship. After all, come Thanksgiving, Christmas, and reunions, you more than likely ate at the same table. A husband wasn't blood, and misdeeds could create a lifetime chasm.

He had no doubt that Clay would eventually make up with Delcia, but this estrangement was casting a pall on her happiness. That wasn't acceptable to Carter. Delcia would soon be his wife and his responsibility. He sighed. He loved the very idea.

Carter considered this his first official deed as a soon-to-be family man.

So the next morning he found himself intercepting Clay at Ryan's house after he saw Ryan's car parked by the camp store.

Nadine had been so nervous about Carter riding on the motorcycle that Paul had insisted that he drive the family car.

Carter parked the '91 Impala in front of the garage.

He walked to the back porch and knocked on the door. The kitchen entrance was more accessible than the front entrance and guests used it more often.

Clay opened the door and grunted when he saw Carter. "Ryan isn't here."

"I came to talk to you."

Clay frowned. "What about?"

"May I come in or would you like to sit on the porch. It's nice out here."

With a closed expression on his face, Clay regarded him a moment and walked angrily to the table on the porch. He pulled out a chair and plopped into the cushioned seat.

Carter settled in a chair across from him.

"You must have heard by now that Delcia and I are getting married in two weeks."

Clay nodded. "I heard."

"I know that you and Delcia have been alienated because of the baby."

"I don't see where that concerns you."

"I beg to differ. I want my wife to be happy."

"And how happy are you going to make her coming from the kind of family you came from? With a brother who's done the unconscionable?"

"I admit that I don't know my natural parents, but that was no fault of mine. I will take responsibility only for what I have done. Not something I had no control over."

"When I was fourteen," Carter continued, "I was very blessed to have the Roberts take me in and raise me as their own. They are good, decent people.

As decent as they come. Not fancy, mind you. But they ran an upstanding home and taught me values and what I needed to function as a man in society."

Clay smirked. "Too bad some of those teachings didn't rub off on your brother."

"I beg to differ." Carter leaned forward. "I'm telling you this in confidence because I don't want the information to leak out just yet." He proceeded to tell Clay about Richard and David. By the time he'd finished, Clay's eyes had widened.

"So you think something's real fishy with that murder?" Clay asked.

"Definitely."

"And your brother's hiding out."

Carter nodded and chose his words carefully. "If the information he gathered is true, it means that his mother felt that she couldn't go home when she discovered she was pregnant. The twin's father was never told. She rented a room in a boardinghouse. Can you imagine what her family must have gone through when she never came home? I'm sure she planned to contact them one day. But she died around strangers, not the people she trusted and loved." Then Carter drove the point home.

"After all is said and done, I'm sure David's natural family would have preferred to have his mother and the twins within the family fold where they knew they were safe. It's a heck of a lot easier to live with. We all make mistakes. None of us are perfect."

Carter pushed his chair back and stood. "I will love Delcia and Ranetta until the day I die, and I consider Ranetta my baby. I'll be adopting her as soon as we marry—with Delcia's permission, of course. Ranetta is a wonderful little girl who has brought joy to many. She's your only grandchild. It's worth celebrating."

He started down the stairs, then glanced at Clay one last time. "If you're a Christian man, sir, you need to have a long discussion with your pastor. I won't have Delcia upset every time you come around. If you can't forgive her and accept her as the loving daughter she is, although I'd love to have you around, I have to do what's best for Delcia." Carter left the threat hanging between them.

Clay hopped out his chair. "You can't keep me from seeing my daughter!"

"She doesn't feel like your beloved daughter right now. I hope we have your blessings." He didn't wait for a reply.

He'd said what needed to be said. The rest was up to Clay.

Carter stopped by Delcia's on his way home. The florist sat among five anxious women: Pauline, Nadine, Wanda, and Willow Mae, with Delcia in the center of it all. She had a desperate look in her eyes.

"I really like the arbor along the wall. We don't need anything too elaborate," Delcia said. "It's an outdoors affair. The flowers are blooming and the grass is pretty and green."

"That reminds me. We need at least two tents." Pauline wrote furiously on her pad.

"I came to steal my fiancée from you ladies," Carter said from the doorway. He'd be the first to admit that he was a coward when it came to getting in the middle of women and their planning.

"You can't do that!" Nadine wailed.

Pauline bristled. "We haven't decided on the flowers yet. Men," she huffed. "You're the one who designated this impossible deadline. You're just going to have to stay out of our way so we can get things done."

"You all can look at the pictures while she's gone. I'll have her back before you know it," he said and hustled Delcia out the house."

Grateful for the reprieve, Delcia breathed a sigh of relief. "You'd think they were getting married with all the carrying-on. My first wedding was very small," Delcia said as they walked across the back lawn. "I think Mom felt cheated. She's certainly making up for it this time."

Carter took her hand in his. "I thought you said it was going to be simple."

"You can forget simple. Where're we going?"

"Along the beach. I just got a call from Stubbs. They're having a funeral for Richard in three days. I think we should go and take Ranetta."

"I agree."

"David called me. He wants to go."

"Of course he would. Richard was his brother."

"It's going to be difficult for Richard's parents seeing him there." Carter steered Delcia toward the edge of the water. He hadn't had time to enjoy his beach lately. He now looked upon it as his own. "Stubbs gave me the Connolys' phone number. They said it was okay. I'm going to call them later."

"I don't know what to say to them."

"You know, when I first thought Ranetta was David's, I wanted to be sure that she got to know family on David's side. Now she has four sets of family."

"She's a well loved little girl."

"Indeed, she is."

Three days later, a whole group of islanders boarded the plane for Seattle: Carter, Delcia, Ranetta, David, Delcia's parents, the Roberts, Harry and Willow Mae, and Dr. Sommars and his daughter Sasha.

David sat beside his new sister and his new father, but David still referred to the Roberts as Mom and Dad.

It was drizzling when they disembarked in Seattle. The Connolys lived in a beautiful development near the university. Many faculty members and students attended the funeral.

David received many shocked stares and the fact that David was a twin had to be repeated several times. All in all the Connolys were very pleased to see them. Most of all on this sad day, they were thrilled with Ranetta.

Fourteen

Mere days from her wedding, Delcia barely had a moment to breathe. Ranetta was currently occupied with chewing a cloth book Carter had given her.

They still hadn't discovered Richard's killer and Delcia and Carter had to steal time to be with each other.

Ryan came to her earlier and offered to walk her down the aisle if she wanted him to. She thanked him, but . . . .

She hung the simple sleeveless gown, with just a touch of pale peach, on the door next to Ranetta's pretty white dress and realized she was going to have to make room for Carter's things. She wished she had more closet space. Come to think of it, a larger master bedroom wouldn't hurt either.

"Have mercy. I'll never get through this wedding," her mother said as she came for Ranetta. "It's noontime already. Time for your nap, sweetheart," she said, lifting the child in her arms. "That gown is gorgeous, Delcia."

"I think so too. I think Carter will be pleased."

"Oh, he'll be pleased with anything you wear," she said and hustled out.

Delcia zipped the gowns in plastic bags and stored them in the closet. Standing in the back of the closet, she was totally shocked to hear her father's voice.

"Delcia . . ."

She swiveled so quickly she almost dropped the dresses. "Yes?" she asked and hung them with extra care. Flicking the light off, she closed the closet door. Then she saw Carter standing in the doorway.

Her father shoved his hands into his pockets. "I'd like a word with you."

She motioned him to the rattan chair. She sat gingerly on the bed, glancing between him and Carter. "What is it?"

Clay took his hat off and twisted the bill in his hands, then he looked at her, his expression as mulish as it had been all year. "I'd like to apologize for my actions this last year. Maybe I shouldn't have judged you so harshly."

"Maybe?" she asked, trying not to glance at Carter.

Clay's jaw tensed. "Definitely."

The air was thick enough to slice with a knife. "I accept your apology," Delcia said.

Carter came further in the room. "Now that I'll soon be a married man, I think peace in the family is a good thing."

Clay grunted and left, almost bumping into Pauline in the hallway. She carried an armful of towels in her arms.

Delcia jumped when she heard the kitchen door slam. "What was that all about?" she asked Carter.

"Just a little family agreement."

"You're a rascal. He would have bitten off his tongue before he admitted he was wrong about anything."

"I don't think so. Lady, I don't know how I'm going to survive three more days."

"You will, just fine," she said, approaching him. "Now give me a kiss. I've barely had you to myself."

Carter dragged her to him and kissed her solidly. In his loving arms, Delcia had a little piece of heaven.

When he came up for air, he said, "It's one thing moving into a house built by another man, but I'm not liking the idea of sleeping in the same bed."

Delcia looked around.

"Do you mind if we went into town to pick out our own set?"

"We could do that or go to the furniture showrooms in Hickory. They have a better selection and it'll be fun."

"Either way's okay with me," he said. "You ever thought of expanding this room? It'll still look in line with the house if we extend it a bit."

"I've wanted a larger master bedroom, even more, a bigger closet."

"Who's the builder in these parts?"

"My cousin . . ."

Carter groaned. "I should have known. Seems like most of the island is related to you."

Delcia shrugged.

"Let's get together with him and see what he can do."

"Okay."

Willow Mae came bursting in Delcia's door an hour later screaming, "Pauline, Pauline!"

Delcia and Pauline ran into the kitchen. "What

234 *Candice Poarch*

is it Willow Mae? Are Dad and Harry fighting again?" Delcia asked her.

Willow Mae clutched her chest. "I just heard that Carter came to the campground where Harry, Clay, Ryan and Mark were putting in trees and getting the lawn all prettied up for the wedding, and he dragged poor Clay off somewhere earlier today. They said Carter was hopping mad about something. Everybody on the island is worried about what he did to your daddy."

Delcia and Pauline glanced at each other and smothered smiles.

"Harry said he deserved whatever he got but I'm not so sure."

"Come on over and have a seat," Pauline said, "before you make yourself sick. Delcia, get Willow Mae a glass of lemonade. It's mighty hot out."

Pauline led Willow Mae to the kitchen table. Once the women were settled with their drinks, Pauline said, "I just saw Clay and Carter an hour ago. Clay left but Carter stayed around for a while. He didn't do anything to him."

"Well, I am sure glad of that. Do you know what the to-do was all about?"

"I haven't got a clue. You know family, they're always fussing about something. Take Harry and Clay for instance."

"You've got the right of it there," Willow Mae agreed and took a sip of her lemonade. "It's enough to tire a body out. You sure you don't know what's going on?"

"Clay didn't say a word to me." That was true enough.

"Well, I've got to be going on, what with all those cakes to make."

"Don't forget to charge the ingredients to my account," Delcia called out as her aunt rose from the chair.

"All right."

Pauline and Delcia saw Willow Mae to her car. As soon as the car rounded the curve the women came into the house and fell into chairs laughing.

"Let me close the baby's room door. The phone calls will start soon," Pauline said after she caught her breath. "For a while I'd forgotten what island life was like."

Delcia and Carter had dinner at the Sea Choice on the mainland after picking up their rings.

"Carter, this diamond is too much," she said as she viewed it under the warm glow of the candlelight.

"Nothing's too much for you."

"You're spoiling me."

"You're mine to spoil."

The intensity in his eyes drove Delcia's heart to racing.

Carter inhaled. "These have been the longest two weeks of my life."

The wound on his head had healed nicely; only a little discoloration was left. "You can say that again. What I really want to know is, what did you do to get my father to apologize?"

"I didn't do anything. Your father loves you."

"I realize that, but he's stubborn to a fault."

"Couldn't tell it by me. Now are we going to

spend this lovely evening discussing Clay Anderson or us?"

"Definitely us."

David had spent the last few days with Sommars. After dinner, Delcia and Carter picked him up to take him to the island with them.

This time when they took the ferry, Carter was very aware of his surroundings. There were only four cars on this midnight excursion. Carter had met the men before through Ryan and they seemed safe enough.

One man had fallen asleep at the wheel. The other two occupants had gone inside.

"I'm going to get a soda and stroll around the deck," David said.

"Okay," Carter said, thinking that David would be safe here. Delcia and Carter stayed in the car, treasuring these last few minutes together. In the dim light, he could see her bare legs. She'd taken to wearing more dresses lately and he liked that.

"Whatever happened with Louise?" she asked.

"I talked to her yesterday. She said that she married Spiedel because the man loved her and that David was lost to her. She said she lost everything after paying her brother's debts."

"When is David returning to his practice?"

"The doctor who's working there now has asked to buy out his portion of the practice. David agreed. He doesn't want to work with them any longer."

"Where will that leave him? He loves his work."

"Sommars wants him to join his practice."

"Does he want to work with his . . . I don't know

what to call him. The Roberts raised him, and Sommars is his biological father."

"Gets complicated, doesn't it? He's considering working with him. The office isn't that far from where he's worked all along. He'll be able to care for the patients he already has. I think it's going to take some time for him to get over everything that's happened.

"I think he really loves Louise."

"There's no accounting for taste, is there? But I think you're right."

"I'm glad he's coming to the island. Being around family will help."

"Let's hope," he said, looking once more to where David stood talking to the ship's crewmen in the well-lit building. He reached for Delcia. "We're not going to spend our time talking, now are we?"

"You've got something better in mind?"

"You bet." He pulled Delcia toward him and covered her mouth with his. Her body was warm and soft in his arms.

He felt her arms around his neck, her fingers delicately stroking his ear as he pressed her closer to him. Carter yearned for the day Delcia would be his. Her soft body pressing against his caused an erection in his jockey shorts, just aching for her. Delcia's hand ran down his chest, his stomach—and then, she touched him.

He moaned. "Damn, I can't take more of this," Carter whispered and kissed her hard. Her hand squeezed the bulge in his pants. His hands slid over her thighs and inched under her dress and slid into her panties to feel the sweet wetness. They caressed, stroked. He ached for her. But he couldn't make love to her when David could return any minute.

"David should be back by now," Carter said in a husky voice.

"I guess," Delcia said, straightening her dress.

Carter looked to where he'd seen David last and a chill ran up his spine. "I'm going to find him. Keep your door locked."

"I'm coming with you," Delcia said, and before he could protest, she was following him. They went inside, but David wasn't sitting in any of the seats.

Carter started to walk around the boat, dragging Delcia with him. A minute later he saw David struggling with a man trying to throw him overboard. Blood was gushing from his side.

"Stay back," he whispered to Delcia before he took after them. Just before he reached them, the man must have realized someone was upon them because he turned and caught David by the shoulder, holding the knife to his neck.

"Stay back," Randall said.

"Randall?" Delcia asked as surprised as Carter.

"What're you doing, man. What's David to you?" Carter said, taking a step closer. The thought that Randall had been hired as a hit man crossed Carter's mind. But who hired him? He had to get him away from David.

"Look, don't do anything stupid. Whatever they're paying you isn't worth killing for."

Randall sneered and nervously wiped a bead of spray from his face. "Sommars' money is enough for me but split three ways, it doesn't go too far."

"What's Sommars to you?"

"My father-in-law."

"It's too late now. We know. You can't kill all three of us and you're not going to get to spend Sommars money. You may as well let David go."

He shook his head and shifted positions, trying to hold the knife on David with one arm and reaching for something with the other. David fell heavily into him.

Carter sprinted toward them.

Both men fell to the deck. The knife flew from his fingers when he tried to catch himself.

Randall reached into his pocket and brought out a gun. Carter reached for the gun hand. They struggled. Carter punched his face, then repeatedly hit his hand against the deck until he released the gun. As Carter reached for the gun, Randall sailed into him. They struggled, then Carter hit him hard. Randall flew back so fast and hard he fell over the railing. When he surfaced in the dark waters, he looked like he was standing still as the boat sped by.

Carter ran to David. Delcia applied pressure to the wound.

"I'll live," David said. "Better stop the boat and throw over a life preserver."

"Let him swim to shore."

"Carter," both Delcia and David warned.

Shit. Carter went inside and grabbed one of the workers, relaying the story.

"Damn. Just about every time you're on this boat something happens," the man said as he called up to the pilot room, then followed Carter outside. "Hope you don't plan to make this a habit."

* * *

"Be back in an hour," Pauline said as she ran out the door. She was on her way to try on her new dress. The seamstress had called to tell her the alterations had been completed.

"I'm going to put sweetie pie here down for a nap." Ranetta's sitter, Jenny Shaw, took Ranetta's bottle from the fridge and snagged the baby from Ryan's arms. Jenny had returned from her daughter's place a few days ago. "Ryan, there's plenty of food in the fridge. Just take what you want." Ranetta gazed from a comfortable position on Jenny's hip.

Ryan stood at the fridge, munching on deviled eggs that Willow Mae had sent over. In addition to baking the cake, she'd brought over pans and pans of food, thinking Delcia wouldn't have the time to cook with all the wedding preparations. The refrigerator was overflowing with food. Harry had mentioned that Willow Mae had been a bit peeved because she hadn't been asked to do more. After all, wasn't she the best cook on the island?

"When will LaToya arrive?" Delcia asked Ryan.

"She isn't coming."

Delcia frowned at him. The woman would be her future sister-in-law, after all. "Why not?"

He piled three deviled eggs, two fried chicken legs and two heaping spoonfuls of macaroni salad onto a plate and shut the door. He carried his plate to the countertop and pulled out a tall bar stool and sat.

"We've called off the wedding."

"Oh, Ryan, I'm so sorry." Here she was blissfully happy, and her brother must be heartbroken. She gazed closely at him. He seemed to be holding up pretty well under the circumstances.

"Actually, I called it off."

"Why?"

He shook his head and held up a chicken leg. "We weren't right for each other. LaToya is a fine looking sister with a body to die for, but after watching you and Carter, I realized that I didn't love her." He dropped the chicken on the plate and wiped his hand on a paper napkin. "I can't base a marriage on looks and hot sex. And I think that's what appealed to me most about her."

"I'm sorry, Ryan, but if it's not right for you, then it won't work. I'm glad you realized that before you married her."

"I came to terms with my feelings when I visited her. I can't leave the island. I love it here, the work that I do. I feel we're building something. It might not be a white collar job, but we offer so much happiness to thousands of people. I feel deep down in my gut that this is the right place for me."

Delcia rounded the countertop, embraced him from behind and kissed him on the cheek. "When the right woman comes along, you'll know. She won't try to change who you are. I think you're wonderful just the way you are. Most of all, I'm glad you'll be here. We're a team."

The kitchen door opened and their father entered, frowning as was his expression more often than not lately. There was a day when he smiled a lot. Seems those days were long gone.

Delcia left Ryan's side. The truce between her father and her was tenuous at best. The pain that he'd caused over the last year wasn't easily forgotten. Even though he'd apologized, it was done grudgingly and Delcia still had nothing to say to him. He wasn't the same man she'd loved through the years. His love came with a price.

"Pauline in the back?"

"She went for some kind of fitting," Ryan said. "You know women and their dresses."

Clay closed the door and glanced at Ryan's plate. "Thought you'd be at work."

"Taking a lunch break," Ryan said as he bit into another deviled egg. Delcia wondered if Ryan had talked Willow Mae out of her deviled eggs. He'd always loved them and whenever he had the appetite for them, even as a kid, he'd ride his bicycle over to her house and persuade her to fix them. A few compliments and she was putty in his hands. "The fridge's full. Help yourself."

Clay shook his head and glanced at Delcia. "Delcia, if you've got a minute, I'd like a word with you."

"Actually, I was getting ready to . . ."

"It's important. Let's take a walk." He opened the door.

Delcia sighed, wondering what he was up to now. She just wasn't up for a confrontation the day before her wedding. Planning this huge ordeal had been stressful enough. Nevertheless, she stood and walked through the door he held for her. He stuffed his hands into his pockets and led the way to the sandy shore.

"What is it?" Delcia finally said. She stepped out of her sandals and carried them in her hands, letting her toes sink into the cool, damp sand.

Clay was still silent as they walked on. Then he cleared his throat. "I know I've been acting . . . well, I've always had your best interest at heart."

"When I follow your rules, that is."

"Your mother and I didn't make rules, just so. They were rules to keep you safe."

"You can't keep me safe. Life isn't always wrapped up in nice safe little packages.

"Some of it we do to ourselves."

"Like, I've made my bed, so I have to sleep in it?" She laughed a hollow sound. "Believe me, you've told me that enough this last year. You didn't need to bring me out here to repeat it. I heard you loud and clear." Delcia glanced at her watch and started to walk away. "I've got a million things to do for tomorrow."

"Hold on, will you?" Clay grabbed Delcia's arm and tugged her back. "I didn't come out here to fight with you."

"Then why are we here?" Delcia snapped.

"Because I wanted to tell you I'm sorry for the way I've acted. I should have been there for you." Clay let go of her arm and turned angrily toward the water.

Delcia stared at her father, speechless. That half-hearted apology he'd made before hadn't been genuine and she knew it. But this—this was different.

"You were always a special little girl. I never had a minute's trouble out of you. Always headstrong. Come hell or high water, you'd go charging after what you wanted. And more often than not you succeeded. But when you had that affair with that young man, it just took me for a loop. I never expected that of you. I wanted you in that perfect little life with the perfect husband and children with a father to raise them just like I was there for you and Ryan with your mother. I couldn't bear the fact that you had set yourself up for this struggle alone. It just wasn't right, it just wasn't meant to be!"

"How dare you say that? Ranetta is the most special thing that ever happened to me."

"I know she's special. I just wanted the best for you."

"I've had and I have the best. Bruce was a wonderful husband. I loved him and Lord knows he loved me. We weren't blessed with children. We both wanted them but it wasn't to be. So when I got pregnant with Ranetta, I was overjoyed. Now Carter has come into my life. I love him. He's different from Bruce. But the love is strong for both of us. I'm blessed to have found love a second time."

"When I got the call that night, Harry said that you were hurt, I thought I'd lost my baby and I'd never get to tell her again how much I love her." He turned to face her.

God, as angry as this man made her, he knew just what to say to pull at the heartstrings.

"When I got here, I didn't know what I'd find. We drove through the night to reach here. We couldn't get a flight out right away, so we just drove. And I didn't know what to say to you when you looked fit as a fiddle. All I could do was thank God for keeping my baby safe. And then the other night on the ferry, you were in danger again. I guess life is too short to carry anger around in the heart. So I'm asking you, Delcia, will you forgive this old fool?"

Tears gathered in Delcia's eyes. She'd thought the two of them would never find their way back to the special relationship that they once shared. They still had a ways to go, but at least he was reaching out.

What more could she ask for? "Of course I'll forgive you."

After all, Delcia thought, *what's love about if not forgiveness?*

Delcia's wedding day dawned sunny and beautiful. That afternoon the gentle winds kept the temperature to a manageable level.

"Mom, I need help with this tie. Dad, you almost ready?" Carter asked.

Nadine clutched her chest and Paul staggered a bit before he caught himself.

"What did you say?" Nadine whispered.

"I said, Mom, may I have some help with this tie?" Carter jerked the tie loose. He was so nervous, he couldn't get it right. As he continued to tug at it, he glanced into the mirror and watched the older couple through his peripheral vision.

Paul sank into a chair. Nadine slowly came forward, wearing a beautiful green semi-formal summer dress and matching heels. With trembling hands, she began to knot the tuxedo tie. A suspicious glassiness appeared in her eyes.

"You gonna be all day with that?" Carter asked.

"You're a rascal, you know that? Telling me this on the most important day of your life. Like to give me conniptions." A tear slid over her lids.

Carter picked her up, hugged her and kissed her on the cheek. "Now, don't you start crying," Carter said. "You'll mess up your makeup after you you've gone through the trouble."

She hit at him. "Put me down, will you, 'fore you mess up your suit and my new dress. Just got the devil in you today. What's the matter with you?" she said, grinning.

Paul finally gathered enough strength to make his way out of his seat.

"Come on over here, Pops," Carter said.

Paul hopped on over there and the men embraced.

"Well, now, this is a fine day, indeed," Paul said, as Carter slung an arm around both his and Nadine's shoulders.

"Will you stay still?" Nadine told him, moving so she could finish his tie, "so I can finish this?"

"Yes, ma'am."

Clay walked her down the aisle to Carter. She wore a beautiful peach silk gown with matching shoes. A single strand of white pearls hung gracefully around her neck.

"Thank you," Carter said to Clay when he left Delcia with Carter. "You're absolutely stunning," he whispered to Delcia.

Her gloved hand trembled in his. He raised her hand to his mouth and kissed her knuckles.

David, decked out in his white tuxedo, cleared his throat and grinned.

"I reckon we best get this on so you two can be together since you can't seem to wait," Rev. Hariston whispered.

They laughed.

And he did get on with it. In no time, they were pronounced man and wife. Well-wishers greeted and hugged them. They posed for the photographer who managed to get a smile out of Clay.

Delcia and Carter looked out on the lawn. Two huge tents were set up, one for the food and the other for wedding guests and the island's band, whose music everyone danced to.

Ryan caught the garter and Wanda the bouquet. Delcia noticed that most of the park's patrons attended the ceremony and stayed for the reception that lasted into the night.

Carter had rented the honeymoon suite in the Sandstone Hotel at Atlantic Beach. From there, they'd fly to Hawaii for a week, a place Delcia always said she'd wanted to visit.

First, however, was the wedding night they'd both been looking forward to. After the bellman opened the door, Carter lifted Delcia into his arms and carried her across the threshold.

She kissed him right there and then. They almost bumped into the man waiting for his tip.

Carter put her on her feet.

"Notice the wine and fruit basket on the table," the bellman pointed out. When he realized no one was listening, he asked, "Do you want the tour?"

"Nope," Carter said, reaching into his pocket. He handed the man some bills.

"Thank you and enjoy your stay." The smiling man made a hasty retreat.

Carter reached for Delcia.

"I've been waiting for this moment forever," he whispered against her skin.

"And so have I," Delcia said and started undoing his clothing as he kissed her. In moments he stood before her with a gorgeous chest covered with dark curly hair. She reached out and rubbed her hands against the contrasting textures of skin, muscle, hair. He drew her close and kissed her.

"Ah, Delcia." Carter's husky voice sent chills of anticipation down her spine. He seemed to consume the very air in the room. "I can't wait another moment."

"Who's asking you to?"

He stepped back from her, but she reached out and stroked one finger from his neck to his pants. Hooking a finger in the waistband she drew him closer and planted a delicate kiss on his neck, his chest, his ear.

His hands glided along her back, her bottom, sliding the silk against her skin. And then he took one long finger and tilted her chin. He crushed his mouth to hers in a hot kiss that nearly buckled her knees. Her body pressed against his so tightly she hardly knew where she left off and he began.

Her world spun as he lifted her into his arms and walked to the bed, depositing her in the center.

Under her watchful gaze, he shucked his clothing and stood nude before her like an African god from another millennium. He was hard and ready.

Then he bent and peeled her clothing from her body. She reached out and touched him. He seemed to vibrate in her hand. He was a generous man—hard all over. A fleeting thought that her tummy wasn't as firm as it had once been flitted through her mind, but the thought evaporated when he spun kisses over her heated body. Every sensory nerve in her body was sensitized and ready by the time he leaned over her and gazed at her as if she were the most precious of jewels.

Then they were one. She tightened her legs and arms around him. She wanted to hold him within her forever—he felt just so damn good—she moaned, pressed his hips closer to her and called out his name. His movements were as graceful as any dancer's as they moved to a magical dance. The tension built, she moved frantically beneath him, needing him so desperately it almost frightened her. And at just that moment when her body crescendoed into fireworks, he rocked her world and snatched her breath away.

"Mrs. Matthews," Carter whispered later, leaning against her.

"Yes, Mr. Matthews." She rubbed her hand against his face.

"You were well worth the wait."

With that secret siren's smile, Delcia rose and kissed him. "And so were you," she said.

Dear Reader:

I visited the North Carolina coast in May when the weather was absolutely beautiful and the food was fabulous. My only regret was that I couldn't spend more time there. I knew it was the perfect setting for *Shattered Illusions*. Very few African-Americans live on islands in that section of the state so I made up my own after the Indians who once lived there. I hope that your journey with Carter and Delcia was equally entertaining.

Intimate Secrets was earmarked the last novel in the Nottoway series, however, every letter that I received requested more on the triplets when they are older. In response to so many kind letters, my fall 2001 novel (untitled for now) will feature Emmanuel Jones and the computer division manager at Blake Industries. The story will begin after the triplet's high school graduation. I think that is such an interesting time for teenagers.

Thank you for so many uplifting letters, and for your support.

You may write to me at:

P.O. Box 291
Springfield, VA 22150

With Warm Regards,
Candice Poarch

ABOUT THE AUTHOR

Reared in a small town in Southern Virginia, best-selling author Candice Poarch portrays a sense of community and mutual support in her novels. She firmly believes that everyday life in small-town America has its own rich rewards.

Candice currently lives in Springfield, Virginia with her husband of twenty-three years and three children. A former computer systems manager, she has made writing her full-time career. Candice is a graduate of Virginia State University and holds a Bachelor of Science degree in physics.

BOOK YOUR PLACE ON OUR WEBSITE AND MAKE THE ARABESQUE ROMANCE CONNECTION!

We've created a customized website just for our very special Arabesque readers, where you can get the inside scoop on everything that's going on with Arabesque romance novels.

When you come online, you'll have the exciting opportunity to:

- View covers of upcoming books

- Learn about our future publishing schedule (listed by publication month and author)

- Find out when your favorite authors will be visiting a city near you

- Search for and order backlist books

- Check out author bios and background information

- Send e-mail to your favorite authors

- Join us in weekly chats with authors, readers and other guests

- Get writing guidelines

- AND MUCH MORE!

Visit our website at
http://www.arabesquebooks.com